Grace
in Old Sodus

ISBN: 978-0-9829756-4-0
Published by:
First School Press
P.O. Box 115
Sodus, Michigan 49126

Edited by Rachel Starr Thomson
Cover Design by Jay Cookingham
Kindle Formatting by Carolyn Currey

Printed in the United States of America

Grace
in Old Sodus

by
Michael Leonard Jewell

Dedication

In memory of Deputy Elton C. Stover, Berrien County Sheriff's Department, who was mortally wounded while responding to an alarm at the Farmers and Merchants Bank in Benton Township, Michigan. Deputy Stover succumbed to those wounds on December 10, 1965, leaving his final call unanswered.

* * *

In memory of my uncle Leonard James Jewell and my nephew Matthew Jon Jewell, who departed this world as little boys only to grow up in heaven at the feet of their Savior.

* * *

In honor of my cousin Doc (Albert Frank Brizendine), who served in the United States Army as a warrant officer and helicopter pilot with Troop D, First Squadron, First Cavalry Division during the war in Vietnam.

On January 28, 1969, near Hue, South Vietnam, Doc piloted a UH-1H (Huey) helicopter in support of a long-range reconnaissance patrol that had become surrounded by a numerically superior enemy force. Unprotected and under intense automatic weapons fire, Doc hovered his aircraft while reinforcing troops disembarked, preventing the patrol from being overrun.

Again, on March 12, 1969, near Thon Thuy Cao, South Vietnam, Doc volunteered to attempt the extraction of six army Rangers surrounded by enemy forces. Under intense automatic weapons fire, Doc directed attacks by helicopter gunships to enemy positions.

Disregarding his own safety, he guided his aircraft over the landing zone and was able to extract the remaining Rangers, then gain necessary altitude and air speed to clear the surrounding trees and fly to safety. For these acts of personal bravery and devotion to duty, Doc was awarded the Air Medal with "V" Device and the Distinguished Flying Cross.

Table of Contents

Prologue
September's Legacy

It was a sunny September afternoon in Hipps Hollow, and Amberley was seated at her place on the back porch swing, carefully reading through a school assignment that was due the next day. Lost in thought, she didn't notice that the evening drew near, and the porch soon fell under the gray shadow of the ancient sycamore tree growing beside the house. Feeling a marked chill, Amberley smiled and zipped up her jacket, pouring herself a cup of hot tea to warm her insides.

Amberley loved September. Nestled like a bookmarker between the dry heat of August and the frosty chill of October, it was a month of transition indeed, reminding her of precious school days gone by—of teachers she had grown to love and cherish, of her pleasant walks with friends along lonesome country roads and shortcuts across flaxen meadows, and of the endless supply of schoolyard bullies.

The memories reached other parts of her life, beyond schooldays and schoolfellows. On one particularly rainy September afternoon, her heart had been filled with unspeakable joy when her father, Sam Bridges, came home safe and sound from his years spent in Vietnam. Only later was she bruised with disillusionment when she discovered he had grown hard and worldly-wise, resorting to alcohol to quench the pain of the war. She was thankful when, in his despair, Sam finally came to Christ and set out to be the man and father she had prayed he would be.

And Mary, Sam's loyal and faithful wife and patient mother to Amberley, unable to have more children of her own, willingly made room in her heart and home for two dear adopted daughters.

This was September's legacy to Amberley. A legacy of change—good and bad. As she looked back upon past days, she recalled the best and willingly forgot those times laced with poverty and disappointment. The little Sodus girl, the dreamer, had finally grown up and was ready to marry her prince and leave home for good, always mindful of a past that perhaps had not treated her quite as badly as she once thought. Amberley understood that once and for all, she must put away the nagging doubts about her future and herself. The question was—could she do it?

One
Karl Has News

It was Monday morning on the big farm in Hipps Hollow, and the Bridges were gathered together in the kitchen for breakfast. The sun had not yet shown itself over the horizon, and the smell of burning apple wood in the small cast-iron stove sweetened the air like perfume, driving the autumn chill beyond the door. Sam was seated in his place at the head of the table buttering his toast when Karl McNee, the hired man, gave his ceremonious rat-a-tat-tat at the door and walked in.

"You folks don't mind if I take breakfast with you this morning?" he said, pulling out a chair. "I just finished the milking and went in to eat with Beth, but she's not feeling well again today. She hasn't been well these last few mornings. I offered to make breakfast for her but she shooed me out of the house saying she wouldn't be able to stand the smell of cooking."

Karl and Beth had been married earlier that year and lived in the cottage beside the big barn that had once belonged to Jeb, the old hired man who had passed away that previous December. Karl had taken his place and now worked for Sam on the big farm. Beth was a registered nurse and worked at the county hospital in Berrien Center. Both had been recently discharged from the army.

Mary, Sam's wife, and Grandma Andrews, her mother, were seated at the breakfast table. Karl seemed oblivious to the possibilities of Beth's symptoms. "I will go and check on her after breakfast, Karl," Mary said with a gentle smile.

"Thanks, ma'am," he said. "I wish you would. I'm a little worried about her. She has just not been herself."

Mary made eye contact with her mother, who returned a broad smile.

After breakfast, Sam and Karl went back to work, and Mary slipped on her jacket. "Girls?" she said to her three daughters. "Go ahead and tidy up while your grandmother and I go see Beth. We'll be back soon."

Amberley and Brenda, Sam and Mary's two older daughters, grinned at each other. "What do you think, Brenda?" Amberley asked, taking a sip of juice.

Brenda nibbled on a strip of bacon she held between her finger and thumb. "I would venture that we are about to have a new addition to the farm—one with two feet this time. Can you think of any names?"

"Don't you think we should let Karl and Beth name their own baby?" Amberley said with a chuckle. "It's only fair."

Lien, their younger sister, sat blinking from her corner of the table. "What are you girls talking about? What baby?"

"Beth, silly! Beth is going to have a baby! Didn't you see the way Ma and Grandma Andrews smiled at each other when Karl talked about Beth being ill?" Brenda answered.

"And Karl doesn't have a clue! He can be such a rube sometimes," Amberley said. "I would love to see the expression on his face when he finds out he's going to be a father. I should think we can expect the little one sometime in late spring. Ooh! I can hardly wait!"

Brenda stood from the table. "Well, let's get these dishes done and get going, or we're all going to be late for school. Lien? Start clearing dishes from the table; put away the food. Amber and I'll wash and dry."

"Brenda, will you forever be so bossy?" Amberley said, shaking her head.

"I'm sorry, but I can't help it. I see something that needs to be done and something just clicks in my head. But you love me one and all, right?" Brenda teased, putting the lid on the butter dish.

* * *

Later that morning, the three sisters having gone off to school and Sam and Karl busy about their duties on the big farm, Dr. Cumberland sat at the kitchen table with Mary and Grandma Andrews. He was serious as he stirred his coffee, deep in thought, and took a first sip. "Ladies, to begin with, Beth is not going to have an easy time of it. She has some complications and will need watching and plenty of rest. I told her to stay off her feet as much as possible. And Karl and Beth's newlywed adventure in that drafty old cabin is not helping matters any. This is not a camping trip in the Smoky Mountains. You must get her out of there. Green moss and mold spores are not good for her or her baby. Beth needs to be where there are people around who can attend to her."

Grandma Andrews's mind went back to that stormy day when Jeb, their old and faithful hired man, sought for help when his wife was giving birth in that same cabin and no one was around to help. She had expressed to Jeb many times her sorrow and regret, but all of the apologies in the world could not change things or erase the guilt she felt. She would not stand by and watch it happen again to Beth and her baby.

"Mary? What about Karl and Beth moving into the house? Jeb's old room is just off the kitchen. That way there would always be somebody here if anything happened. I know that Karl doesn't want to be a burden, but Sam can square it with him and make him understand that it's for the best." She ended emphatically, her fiery old resolve showing through.

"I think that would be a wonderful idea, folks," Dr. Cumberland interrupted, helping himself up with his bamboo cane. "I'll let you work out the details, and I'll stop by later in the week to check on Beth." He smiled and pressed his hat upon his head as he walked to the door. "If you need me sooner, you know you just have to call."

At the door, he turned again to face them. "Why don't you just tear down that old shack? It harbors too many bad memories and isn't fit for people to live in." Then, raising his cane to wave good-bye: "So long folks; my pardon for speaking my mind."

"Good morning, Doctor, and thank you," Mary said, closing the door behind him.

Mary looked at her mother. "Well, I'll speak with Sam after lunch. It will be up to him to sell the idea to Karl. I'm sure Beth would rather be in the house with us if she had her druthers."

Two
Billy Gussette

On the way to the local college they attended, Amberley and Brenda dropped Lien off at River School and drove away in the red vintage Studebaker that had been a gift from dear Mrs. Holloway, the wealthy widow from King's Landing. It was a chilly morning, and the fog from the warmer river water moved in to join the dew in the low places surrounding the school, reflecting the brilliant sunlight as if it shone through a magnifying glass. Several students were already milling about, so Lien looked for a place to sit down. Wiping away the moisture from one of the swings with a small cloth she kept with her for that purpose, she took a seat in the chill air, her face engulfed in the plume of her breath.

Lien was all alone as she looked about her and saw the older girls standing next to the building, chatting with their friends. She smiled to herself and imagined the girls smugly looking down their collective noses at her. This was high school, and Lien was expected to act like everyone else, with rubber-stamp clothing and behavior. But she was in no great hurry to grow up. Even though she was becoming a woman and the world looked both different to her and differently at her, she would let maturity and adulthood come to her rather than seek it out. She would "put away childish things" at her own pace. Winter would soon be here, and there would be no more sitting on swings or hovering near the red-brick wall, so Lien intended to enjoy these last few days of autumn in her own way, and after a long Sodus winter, she would consider the virtues of standing against the building, chumming with the other girls.

Lien did not have many close friends outside of her adopted family. Some people, it seemed, were still reluctant to warm up to the little orphan girl from Vietnam, and she marveled at the expressions on their faces when she spoke perfect, unbroken English without a trace of an accent. Even some of the classmates she had known for years were not completely comfortable around her, and she could always detect that little thing when they were together, like the proverbial elephant in the room. Others she met from time to time spoke to her in Pidgin English as if they unconsciously believed she really spoke that way.

As Lien kicked the dirt under her swing, she noticed Billy Gussette rounding the corner up the hill on River Road. She knew what it was to be poor, but Billy was probably poorer than she had ever been, even when she lived in the fishing village in Vietnam. He had no bicycle and had to walk to school every day even in the bitterest weather. Billy lived with his widowed mother down the alley from the Bridges' old house in town. Mrs. Gussette's life had not been a happy one. She had never gotten over the death of her husband, a deputy sheriff who was murdered just before Christmas many years ago while attempting to foil a bank robbery. She had to work odd jobs to keep food on the table. Things had looked up briefly when she was hired to work at Berrien General Hospital, but rumors were in the air that her job might soon be eliminated. Lien did not know what they would do for money.

Lien watched Billy approach and waved. Billy was one of her true friends. He seemed to regard her small, delicate Asian features as attractive and not as a curiosity. Perhaps it was because he was sort of an oddball himself and never popular with the other students. In a way, they were both misfits in a world that regarded circumstances and physical differences as the most important things in life. Maybe that was what had driven them together and made them pals. She didn't care. He was short and stocky but tough as nails, as anyone who dared pick on him found out. He was roughly handsome and had a nice smile, and it made her heart happy to see him every day.

"Hey Billy," Lien called out, greeting him with a big smile. "I saved you a seat." Billy grinned, sitting next to her among rows and rows of empty swings. Dropping his books on the ground in a pile, he said, "You're here early. But then you usually are. Wish I had your character."

Lien smiled. "It's easy to have character with two older sisters fussing at you to get ready. But I don't mind. I don't like being late." Lien looked at Billy's face and noticed that he was squinting and favoring his left eye. "Oh Billy, you have a black eye! You've been fighting again!" She pulled off her mitten and tenderly touched the puffiness above his cheek.

"It's no big deal. Just a little scrap I got into the other day. If I take real good care of it, it might last for a week or more," Billy said with his toothy grin.

"Billy, why would you ever want to go around with that thing on your face?"

He gripped the chains of the swing and let his feet sweep out before him. "It's all mental, you see. If the guys see me sporting this shiner, they'll think twice before picking on me. I may get to go a whole week without having to belt somebody for some smart remark."

Billy had been teased and ridiculed by the bigger guys ever since Lien could remember. He was a bully magnet to be sure and got beat up a lot, but he never backed down. He would ball up his fists and that was that. But now he was sixteen, and manhood was fast approaching, where this kind of thing would be handled by the police and not the school principal. It scared Lien to think about.

"Billy, please stop fighting! You are going to get hurt bad or end up putting someone in the hospital. Your mother doesn't need this, and if you have a police record, you won't be able to get on the sheriff's department. Besides, your father was a deputy. What would he say if he were here?"

Before the last words fell from her lips, Lien realized she had gone too far. Billy turned his head, gazing off in silence. She had used the memory of his father against him, as undoubtedly many had done before in their attempts to keep this unruly boy in line.

"Billy?" she said, turning his face toward her with her delicate hand. "I'm so sorry. I promise I will never do that again. I had no right." She leaned over and bumped her head against his shoulder playfully. "Still friends?"

Billy looked at the ground and smiled. "I could never be mad at you, Lien. You are my best friend and the only one who really cares about me. Well, other than my mother." He grinned. "I will try my best to avoid a fight and not let them boys get my goat." Just then, the school bell rang, announcing classes were about to start. Leaving the swings, the two walked toward the red-brick schoolhouse to begin their day together.

Three
Getting Settled

It was Tuesday afternoon, and the big house was a buzz of activity. It was moving day, as Sam had convinced Karl that it was best for Beth and their forthcoming baby to be in the big house where someone would always be near. Soon, Jeb's old room off the kitchen was ready to be occupied once more, and whatever did not fit was carried up into the attic. The inside of the room was as large as the old cottage, with enough space for a small couch along a corner bay window so Beth and Karl could have a sitting area. Now Karl could go about his duties on the farm with confidence, knowing that Beth was in the house where help was but a shout away.

"Sam?" Karl said as he lifted a heavy box onto his shoulder. "You can take rent out of my pay for the new digs."

"We are happy to have you both with us, Karl, and nothing brightens up life better than a new baby in the house. Now let's hear no more of that," Sam answered.

Dr. Cumberland believed that Beth's pregnancy might be a difficult one, and so far her experience agreed with him. She soon found that standing on her feet for hours and doing her rounds at the hospital were not agreeing with her—a new experience for a rambunctious former army nurse, accustomed to doing her job under combat conditions. Unable to do her work at the hospital, Beth had been forced to take a leave of absence. She was glad to be out of the old cottage and would try to make herself as useful as possible in her new surroundings.

It was finally suppertime, and everyone gathered around the long table in the kitchen. It almost seemed like Thanksgiving. The only person missing was Hank, Amberley's fiancé, who was pulling one of his monstrously long and weary shifts at the hospital. He was looking forward to soon completing his residency so that he and Amberley might get married. Amberley's dream was to have a double wedding with Brenda and Joe. Brenda would certainly go to live on the Schenkle farm with Joe and his mother in that wide-spot-in-the-road known as Shanghai, but Hank's plans were still unsettled. He had received offers from several large hospitals all over the country and even an inquiry from Canada. Hank's family was from Chicago and wealthy and their influence made Hank's prospects as a doctor limitless, but feeling the tug and pull from several directions, he was having a difficult time deciding what he wanted to do.

As everyone talked and laughed, Amberley grew quiet, thinking of Hank and of the future. His absence tonight felt a symbol of her fears. She only saw Hank several times a week, and when she did, he was usually exhausted. Sometimes when they spoke he would nod off, and she couldn't tell if he was just that tired or if she was unable to keep his interest. Hank was always sweet with her and seemed glad to see her, but that old ghost kept creeping back, telling her that her handsome, wealthy doctor could have anyone he wanted, and why should he waste his life with a redheaded, unsophisticated country girl from Podunk Michigan?

She hadn't spoken with anyone about it, but Amberley had not been feeling well lately. She had contracted a rare disease several years back that almost took her life, and her recovery had been a long, tenuous road. She feared that several recent unexplained bouts of weariness and weakness meant her old malady might be coming back. Last Christmas she had been so happy, with Hank's parents visiting from Chicago and the thoughts of a bright future ahead as his wife. But if she was relapsing, that might never happen. Amberley would keep it a secret and take it day by day, and perhaps the Lord would heal her. Whatever happened, she was not going to be an unnecessary burden around Hank's neck. He was a good man and a brilliant, gifted doctor. If she could not truly be an asset to him as his wife, she would let him go.

Karl and Beth burst into laughter over something Grandma Andrews said, and Amberley managed to smile and laugh along with them. She forced her thoughts away from Hank but found that she just couldn't enter into the conversation. Her mind drifted to her writing, waiting for her upstairs. She had always wanted to be the author of a great novel, and she wrote whenever she could, sometimes seated at her old wicker desk before the large window in her bedroom or in her favorite place, the swing on the back porch. She had recently written and published a magazine article for which she received pay, and she'd thought that writing a book would be the same, only take a while longer. She envisioned the process as sort of a magical journey where inspired words were imparted to paper, allowed to flow together and congeal into paragraphs and chapters like quicksilver, culminating in a wonderful tale that the world would clamor to read. She soon discovered, however, that writing a book was far more complicated, intimidating, and frustrating than penning an article. As the pressure increased for her to get it done, her words grew stale and she was forced to set the manuscript aside for weeks at a time until her interest was rekindled. The whole experience seemed to rob her of the joy she sought from it, and she had discovered in the end that writing was "work" just like everything else.

Amberley frequently phoned her old teacher and Beth's aunt, Margaret Davison, for advice and encouragement. She was always helpful and took time from her busy life to encourage her former pupil, but Amberley realized that if the book was ever to be completed, she would have to get busy and do it herself.

She had always wanted to write a book about her life in Sodus, but she found that it was hard to know what to put in and what to leave out. Loath to pen a "tell all" book that would only hurt people by uncovering personal things best kept in the shadows, she mostly wanted to honor God by showing what He had done for them as a family. And as she forced herself to write, Amberley found that her anxieties over Hank could be temporarily put on a back burner to simmer.

* * *

Night had fallen on the big farm, and the sleepy residents of the big house had retired to their beds. Karl and Beth closed the door to their room off the kitchen and sat together with their tea on the small couch before the bay window. Karl unlatched one side of the casement, pushing it open to let in the night air. As the couple sat in the silence, illuminated only by a small candle on the dresser, they could hear the eerie wail of a screech owl perched in a distant tree. Taking a sip of her cup, Beth leaned her head against Karl's shoulder. "Do you think we are taking too much advantage of Sam and Mary's kindness?" she asked. "Does it bother you?"

Karl lifted his chin to allow Beth to snuggle closer. "If I think about it too much, it does. They would give us the buttons off their coats if we asked them. I realize, though, that this is all temporary until the baby is born. Hopefully, and soon, we can figure a way to build a house on the land Jeb gave us for Christmas."

Beth set her cup down on the small table in front of them. "I hope so too, Karl—but I do love it here, and I love these people, and the sounds and sights and smells of the farm. I will certainly miss it."

"I know what you mean," Karl said. "But we'll still be living close by, and besides, we need to start a heritage of our own. Let's concentrate on our baby for now and pray that the rest of things will take care of themselves. There is no rush. We don't have to move out today or tomorrow."

Karl stood up to close the window as Beth stirred from her place. "Let's get some sleep. I'm tired and have an early morning. Besides, I've had enough of Mr. Owl for one night."

Four
Billy Makes a Dark Decision

The week had passed, and Friday morning came. Lien was always a little sad during the weekends because it wouldn't be until perhaps Sunday in church that she would see Billy again, if at all. He hadn't been coming as faithfully as when he was younger, and Lien could see a pattern developing. Soon, perhaps, he would start skipping church altogether and playing hooky from school, and as they drifted apart, their friendship would grow cold.

Lien waited in her usual swing and watched for Billy to come walking down the road, but he didn't come. Maybe today was the beginning of that day she so dreaded. The bell finally rang, and she could no longer wait. *Where is Billy?* she thought as she stood up to walk inside, pondering all the possible reasons he might not come to school that morning. Lien stood inside the door for a moment, hoping for a glimpse of him hurrying down the road from Sodus, when she saw an old faded black pickup truck chugging up in front of the school. Blue smoke from its tailpipe and the stench of burning oil filled the air. The passenger door opened, and to Lien's surprise, Billy got out. The driver was an older man with long silver hair whom she didn't recognize, and he quickly sped away.

Billy had something in his hands that appeared to be an old cloth feed sack with the handle of a small spade sticking out. He looked around with a cautious expression as the exhaust smoke and gray dust from the truck lingered about him. Then he walked to the edge of the schoolyard, bent down, and hid the items under a thick evergreen shrub. Lien did not understand what she was seeing, but she could tarry no longer. She had to get to her homeroom.

Seated at her place by the window, Lien thought about Billy's suspicious behavior and decided she was going to confront him about it at lunchtime. If he was doing something he shouldn't, she was going to find out and try to talk him out of it. Billy didn't have a dad like her Sam to go to. He only had his mother, and she was over her head in debt, poverty, and worry, unable to properly take a tough boy like Billy in hand.

School was dismissed for lunch hour, and Lien and Billy made their way to one of the picnic tables along the rear of the building. The sun was bright, and the air had warmed considerably from that morning. Lien opened up her lunch box, which held a thermos of hot chocolate, a chicken-salad sandwich, two boiled eggs, and a piece of apple pie. Billy reached into the pocket of his ragged coat and took out a crumpled wad of waxed paper—stained and looking like it had been used over and over several times before. With nothing to drink, he unwrapped his crude sandwich: two slices of thick white bread with a slab of government surplus cheese in between. Lien's mouth dropped open when she noticed several spots of dark blue mold on the crusts of the bread.

"Oh Billy!" Lien exclaimed. "Please don't eat that!" Without thinking, she reached out and snatched the sandwich from Billy's hand as he prepared to take a bite. "Here!" she said, handing him her chicken sandwich. "Billy, you don't have to eat moldy bread!"

Billy looked surprised at his little friend's reaction. "Sorry, Lien. I guess I didn't see it. Ma baked this about a week ago, and I hadn't noticed that it's started to turn. The cheese should still be good, though."

Lien was fighting back tears. "Billy, I have plenty in my lunch box. Please share it with me. I can't abide you eating moldy bread and cheese." Billy smiled and took a bite out of her sandwich. As Lien watched him eat, she took a hard look at his rough appearance and thought about that first night in this place—that rainy, cold night she and her parents had spent in the darkness of Hipps Hollow. Fresh from Vietnam and swindled by their unsavory contacts in Chicago, she and her parents had been dumped off in Sodus Township without ceremony. Taking shelter in the dark woods along the river, Lien's mother attempted to make a fish stew, when the spotlight from a police car startled them and the precious food was wasted all over the forest floor. Her Vietnamese parents had died soon after in a terrible fire, and God brought her to live with the Bridges family. Her beginning had been a tragic one, but the Lord had turned it around for her good.

Billy was not all alone like she had been, but his poor mother still struggled to provide for him properly. Lien had not really scrutinized her friend's general appearance lately, thinking of him as just another typical dusty country boy, but now she realized that these were the same clothes she had seen him wearing almost every day that week. Perhaps they were all he had.

Lien felt a tear track down her cheek as her heart broke. She loved Billy—she finally admitted it to herself. She made up her mind then and there that she would always pack enough lunch for them both and never miss a day of school ever, lest he go hungry.

Billy finished the sandwich. "Aren't you going to have some, Lien?" he asked. "I don't want to eat all of your lunch."

Lien smiled sweetly and said, "I'll have one of the boiled eggs and a sip of cocoa. I'm really not that hungry—a big breakfast, you know."

As Billy took his last bite of pie, Lien closed her lunch box and cleared her throat. "Billy, please don't be mad at me, but I saw you get out of that man's truck and hide the feed sack under the shrub. What's going on?"

Surprised, Billy looked into her eyes. "I guess I can't hide anything much from you, Lien. Before I say anything, though, you must promise me that you will not tell anyone. Promise?"

Her heartbeat quickened. How could she keep a secret if it turned out to be something harmful? "But Billy!" she protested.

"No, you must promise, as you are my best friend," Billy said emphatically. "I can't tell you unless you promise!"

Lien paused for a moment and then, rolling her eyes, she raised her right hand and said, "Okay. Scout's honor!"

Billy smiled. "Look, you know things haven't been going very good with me and my mother. She lost her job at the hospital, and not a lot of money has been coming in. I met this guy in town the other day, the man you saw me with this morning, and he is willing to pay me fifty dollars for some Indian artifacts if I can get them."

Lien furrowed her brow. "What Indian artifacts?"

"You've heard of the old Indian graveyard in Poor Boy's Woods down River Road? Well, there is supposed to be a stone there—a special stone carved out by an Indian chief many years ago. It's worth lots of money to some collector out of state. If I can get it for him, he will pay me. My mother and I need that money real bad."

Lien couldn't believe what she was hearing. "Billy, please don't do it. Those old woods are a horrible, frightful place, and how can you think of taking things from someone's grave? There is quicksand and all kinds of scary stuff down there. There's got to be a better way. You're a Christian and know better. Let's talk to Pastor Mitchell about it!"

Billy stuck out his jaw. "My mind's made up, Lien. It will be all right. I talked to some of the old-timers in town, and I think I know about where the graveyard is. I can be in and out before the sun sets. I told my mother I would be going to a football game after school today and would be late coming home so she won't be looking for me."

Lien was shocked. "Billy—you can't lie to your own mother! Please don't go."

But as the words fell from her mouth, she knew that Billy was not listening. He saw this as a way of getting some desperately needed cash to help his mother, and no one could talk him out of it.

Later that day, when her sisters picked her up in front of River School, Lien looked out the rear window at Billy, who had already started his long trek south along River Road to the gloomy woods that were even deeper and darker than Hipps Hollow. She wanted to tell Sam. He would know what to do, but she had made a solemn promise of secrecy to Billy and must keep her word, especially after scolding him for lying to his mother.

Oh Lien! What have you done? she wondered as the figure of Billy got smaller and smaller and then disappeared from view.

Five
The Gazebo in the Woods

Saturday morning was overcast, and the little bit of wind off Lake Michigan put a chill in the air. Amberley stood at her bedroom window in the dark, watching as the eastward horizon began to glow against the dark blue of the night. Hurriedly, she bathed and dressed, descending the stairs with silent footfalls to stand guard by the stove lest the heating tea kettle whistle and wake up the house. Quietly, she sat with her cup of tea at the kitchen table until a pair of headlights made their way down the long driveway to the house. On her feet in a moment, she rushed to open the door and waited at the top of the porch steps. The car door opened, and out stepped Hank, who had just finished a long shift at the hospital.

"Well, you certainly are the prettiest thing I've seen all week. I might just take you out sometime if you can get permission from your mother," Hank said with a wide grin as Amberley threw her arms around his neck and kissed him.

"Why would I need permission?" she asked as Hank twirled her around.

"Well, I'm not sure she would approve of you sneaking out of the house at this time of the morning with some strange guy," Hank replied, opening the door to the passenger side of the car.

Amberley laughed. "More likely she wonders if this strange guy and I are ever going to get married." A jab of sadness hit her even as she let the words out. She meant the comment in jest, but down deep inside, it was a serious question. Excitement overrode the feeling, however: she hadn't seen Hank for several days, and he was taking her out for breakfast and a drive in the country.

A quick turn and up the driveway to Hipps Hollow Road and then north took them to the Blue Star Highway that snaked along the Lake Michigan coast. The sun was burning brightly through a pasture of clouds like so many white puffy sheep as they crossed the line into Van Buren County, and in a few more miles, they were at a rustic old restaurant along the lake shore. There were no other cars visible as they pulled into the tree-lined, red-brick parking lot. "We must be early, Hank. No one else seems to be interested in breakfast," Amberley commented.

"Must be," Hank said with a slight smile. "That's all the more for us."

The waitress showed them into a small room with a large window overlooking the beach and water. Except for several dimly burning oil lamps around the room, the window was the only source of light. The waitress took their order and brought coffee, leaving them to the seclusion and the view. Amberley was surprised when upon returning, the waitress addressed Hank as "Mr. Wheeler." Hank seemed not to notice and reached over to hold Amberley's hand.

26

"How did the waitress know your name?" Amberley asked.

Hank looked into her eyes. "We are her only customers for the next two hours. She was just being personal and polite. I reserved this place so we could spend time alone. I figured I owed you."

"You mean this room?"

"Not exactly," Hank answered with a slight smile again. "I reserved the whole restaurant. It was easier that way and less chance of us being bothered."

"How much . . . ? No, I don't want to know," she said, closing her eyes and shaking her head in amazement. Amberley gazed out the window, watching the waves slap against the shore. She was just beginning to realize how much power there was in having money. She had planned to spend some time talking about the wedding and their future, but strangely, she couldn't force herself to bring it up now. Truth was, she felt intimidated — the little country waif from Sodus in love with a wealthy Chicago doctor. She felt like an insect on the wall, peering out into the room, watching everything unfold. How surreal it was and how reluctant she felt to speak with Hank about things they should be freely discussing. What was Hank waiting for? Was he expecting her to bring it up, or was he just avoiding the subject? Either way, what a tragedy of cross-purposes this was turning out to be.

* * *

Brenda stood at the table in Maudie Schenkle's steamy kitchen in Shanghai, quickly peeling the blanched skins from the next batch of peaches and removing the pits. There was hardly a place to step, the floor was so cluttered with boxes of fruit jars and baskets of peaches. Fruit flies hovered everywhere as Brenda wiped the perspiration from her red face with her sleeve. Maudie, Joe's mother, packed the awaiting fruit jars with halved peaches, pouring in thick, hot syrup and placing a maraschino cherry on top. The pressure cooker hissed away on the stove as Joe set the previous batch of sealed jars on the porch outside to cool.

Sweltering in the heat, Brenda wondered if it wouldn't be cheaper to just buy canned peaches at the local discount store, but this was the way country folk had always done it, and she wasn't about to buck conventions. She didn't want her future mother-in-law to think she was lazy or helpless or unwilling to do what was necessary and expected to feed her family.

"We're almost done, Brenda. I never cottoned much to canning, but it is something that must be done," Maudie said, dabbing her dripping forehead with the towel draped over her shoulder.

Brenda was surprised. "I thought you liked this sort of thing, Mrs. Schenkle. Joe always raves about your canned peaches with toast on a cold winter's morning."

Maudie smiled. "I know, and so did my late husband, but it's a powerful lot of work and I'm getting too old for it. Glad you could help, dear. When I was a little girl, the woman of the house was expected to fill the larder with canned goods. My mother didn't consider herself as having done her duty if she didn't make up at least a thousand jars a year."

Maudie leaned against the counter and stretched her back. "We canned everything back in those days, and not just fruits and vegetables and jams and jellies. Ma would can anything that would fit into a jar: soups, stews, dumplings and chili, whole chickens in the two-quart jars, all kinds of meats, including venison, and even fried sausage patties in their drippings. I had ten brothers and sisters, poor relatives and neighbors, and Ma made sure everyone was fed. She baked bread twice a week and biscuits ever' morning. When the Depression hit in the thirties, we hardly noticed it because we raised and preserved our own things." Maudie sounded wistful as she finished, "Those were great days."

* * *

That afternoon in Sodus Township was sunny and bright. The shadows from the fog and clouds of the morning vanished away, and now it was clear and dry and well into the warm seventies. The big farm was almost deserted, and Lien had decided she would take the opportunity to go for a walk alone to visit her favorite place in the hollow.

She thought about Billy as she finished up a few chores first, knowing that she had done a foolish thing by promising to keep his adventure quiet. If she had felt free to speak with her father about it, he might have been able to steer Billy away from doing something so dangerous. On the other hand, if she had refused to keep his secret, she risked losing his trust and friendship. What was she to do?

But surely it was all over by now. She had heard nothing, and Billy must be safe and secure at his little house in Sodus.

Lien took her bath and went to the large wooden wardrobe in the corner of her room. There, hanging in a plastic dry cleaner's bag, was a beautiful blue-and-white dress called an *ao dai,* the traditional dress worn by Vietnamese women and girls. It was a gift from Mai Lee Wheeler, the wife of Hank's older brother Richard. Mai Lee had visited last Christmas, and being Vietnamese herself, she had struck a special bond with Lien. They had become fast friends and pen pals. Carefully preserved in a box on top of the wardrobe was a *non la* or leaf hat that had belonged to her mother, salvaged from the fire years ago.

Lien had purposed that once a year she would wear this dress and hat and visit the place in the hollow where her parents had died saving her life. Quickly dressing, she stood before the mirror, smiling at how delicate and girly she looked in contrast to the usual appearance of a farmer's daughter. She pulled up her dress slightly to look at her feet and wiggle her toes. She decided not to wear shoes but to walk to the hollow in her bare feet so she would remember who she really was—an orphan girl from a poor little village on the other side of the world.

Taking her thermos of hot tea and her special teacup along in a cloth bag, she exited the kitchen door and headed to the path for the hollow. She hoped she wouldn't meet anyone on the way. What she was doing today was very personal and certainly would not be understood by strangers, who might think she was being dramatic.

The autumn leaves in the bright sunshine made the woods light and airy, unlike the heavy, green darkness of summertime. The path was dry but not so dry that she kicked up dust as she walked. Lien loved this time of year. The insects were less bothersome than in summer, except for the noisy cicadas buzzing in the trees. She could see the St. Joseph River just beyond, and the tomboy in her wished she was fishing with Sam . . . but today she must think of other things.

She stopped, letting her hat fall back onto her shoulders, and holding her hand to shield her eyes, she gazed off into the deep and distant hollow. There, like a fairy castle, was the gazebo Sam and Karl had built for her to honor her parents. It was painted glossy white, with a white lattice, and was screened in to keep out the squirrels and other creatures that might want to take up residence there. Sam had made her a small garden around it like he had seen in Saigon. It was charming and beautiful, with bamboo and other tropical plants and flowers, some that had to be dug up each fall and replanted each spring lest they be killed by Michigan's harsh winters. It was her special place. Even though Sam and Mary were her parents now, they did not want her to forget her heritage. She was grateful.

A small wooden bench marked the place where her father had built a hut to shelter his family when she was just a seven-year-old girl many years ago. Lien meandered down to the gazebo and took a seat on the bench.

As Lien poured her tea, she quietly reflected on her early days, remembering the federal judge who had ordered her returned to Vietnam. When all possible avenues had been exhausted to keep her in America, Sam had told her the story of the Lord Jesus in her own language and given her the precious Vietnamese Bible. Then, when all seemed lost, she had been rescued at the last moment by Sam's friends in the Special Forces while on a plane in the Philippines bound for Vietnam. From that moment on, she had belonged to Sam and Mary Bridges. She would never forget the miracle that brought her here to Sodus.

* * *

The sun was deceiving. Although bright and pleasingly warm, its arc across the sky was perceptibly shorter than in summer. The shadows in the hollow had already lengthened, and a hint of chilling currents could be felt crawling along the floor of the woods. Lien poured her last bit of tea and gathered her things to leave.

Hearing the snapping of a dry stick further up the path, she turned to look. It was Karl McNee. Karl had not warmed to her when he first came to work for her father. He was also a Vietnam veteran and an army Ranger, and when he left the military and came to live in Sodus, he discovered that he still carried a lot of baggage from the war. Lien's presence had troubled him. With its stormy beginning, their friendship had been a long time in coming. As she watched him approach, she stood up, wondering what his reaction would be to see her dressed in her Vietnamese clothing.

"There you are!" he said, lifting his hand to wave. "Your ma thought you might be here. She wants you to come back to the house. Your friend Billy Gussette didn't come home last night and is still missing. Sam has gone to help the sheriff find him."

Karl's words gripped her heart as she nodded and quickly gathered her belongings. "By the way, Lien, you look very nice. I was always fond of the beautiful dresses the ladies wore in Vietnam," Karl said with a smile.

"Thank you, Karl," she said, but the smile faded from her face as she thought of Billy, and her stomach began to flutter uneasily, as if it were full of hundreds of wiggly, crawly things. She perceived that now she was going to have to answer for her misguided vow. And as she and Karl walked up the path leading to the big farm, she was struck by words from the book of Job—*The thing which I greatly feared is come upon me!*

Six
Sam Learns His Place

Sam stood on the brow of the deep ravine with Chief Jorgans of the Sodus police and a few of the county deputies, waiting for the sheriff to arrive. He wore his characteristic tiger fatigues, web gear, and razor-sharp knife, sheathed handle down from his shoulder strap that he had worn in Vietnam.

Steadying himself against a gray beechnut tree, Sam scanned the shadowy forest floor that stretched along the St. Joseph River shore before him. Adjusting his binoculars, he peeked over the rim of the ravine, which was perhaps the original shoreline of the river many hundreds of years ago, into what seemed like the entrance to another world. These woods were indeed well hidden, especially in the summertime, and most people who passed down River Road didn't even realize the place was there. The sides of the ravine were very steep, in some places sheer, and the trees and brush so thick that in places one had to zigzag as he walked to even penetrate them.

At the center of the woods was a murky green swamp laced with fallen dead timbers, peat bogs, and a network of creeks and streams with brown water and quicksand. With its crisscrossed channels, it was remarkably like the bayous in Louisiana where Sam had once trained in the Special Forces. It was not a good place to go by yourself unless you were trying to get injured or lost. One might not be found for days, if at all, and dead, the turkey vultures would have you stripped down to the bone in just a few hours. There were bobcats, coyotes, and snakes, and some had even reported the occasional mountain lion and black bear. Indians had lived here, and an Indian cemetery was rumored to be nearby, but its exact location was unknown, lost to the vagaries of time. Sam had lived in Sodus most of his life, but like everyone else, he avoided these forbidding woods along the southwestern corner of Sodus Township. There was no good reason to ever go down there.

Mrs. Gussette had reported Billy missing that morning, and the road deputies with a tracking dog were able to locate his scent. It had led them to this spot, where they believed Billy had entered the woods. Now the sheriff had taken up the search, and Sam looked forward to meeting him and rendering any help he could.

The slamming of a few car doors told Sam that the new sheriff had arrived. As Sam walked over to greet him, he couldn't get over how young the man looked. He was accustomed to dealing with Sheriff Warner, who was his senior, but this fellow looked like a college freshman.

Sam held out his hand for a shake and was surprised when the young sheriff ignored his gesture, instead standing fast with his arms akimbo at his side. Finally, to preserve some dignity, Sam dropped his hand and folded his arms against his chest as the two men faced off in silence.

The sheriff broke the standoff with a short greeting and a blunt, accusatory look at Chief Jorgans. "So you're the famous Sam Bridges I've heard so much buzz about? Green Beret and Vietnam, they tell me. Well, many people are former military these days, aren't they? I was a lieutenant in the air force myself. I think we can find this boy, Mr. Bridges, without any outside help. This is a police matter and should be conducted by police officers. Sorry you had to come out for nothing. Whoever called you in should have checked with me first."

Then the young sheriff glanced at his watch and turned to his men. "Let's get set up over there and get out that map. It's early yet, and with the tracking dogs and a little luck, we might be able to find this kid before suppertime."

Sam was surprised and frankly disappointed by the sheriff's snub. He had always been treated with great respect by those in law enforcement. He could feel the heat rising in his face as he watched the young sheriff and his men assemble a small tent and begin perusing a map of the woods on a chart board. He was accustomed to being in on the planning, giving advice and directing the search. This was the type of thing for which he had been trained, and old Sheriff Warner had always invited him to lead the charge, but this man . . . !

"I was a lieutenant in the air force myself"! Sam thought, still hearing the sheriff's sarcasm ringing in his ears. *And since when is finding a lost boy just a 'police matter'?*

Feeling the sting of the moment, Sam walked over to his pickup truck and started the engine. "Shave tail!" he muttered under his breath as he returned to his farm in Hipps Hollow.

* * *

Sam said little during supper, and after taking a last swallow of coffee, he plucked his hat off the peg on the wall and let the screen door slam behind him as he left the house. Saddling one of the horses in the barn, he set out alone for the path leading to the hollow. Deep in thought, he ruminated over his past and reflected upon the hard life he had lived in his early days and the road that had led him to where he was now. Leaving Sodus for the first time as a mere kid, he had been quickly influenced and transformed in the strange new worldly environment of the army. Then came the Special Forces and combat in Vietnam, giving him the pride and self-assurance he needed to accomplish almost anything he put his hand to. But with all his training and experience came a stuffy confidence and conceit, causing him to believe he didn't need anybody else—especially God. Sam had looked down his nose at those who relied upon their faith and regarded them as weak and needing a crutch—his wife included. As the Holy Spirit tugged at his heart day by day, his resistance drove him to the bottle for escape, hurting his family and straining his marriage. Finally, broken inside, Sam had yielded in faith to Christ for salvation, relying upon His love and grace. It had transformed him and put him on the path to becoming the man God had always wanted him to be.

Strands of salt and pepper now frosted his temples, and the occasional twinges and aches in his joints told him he was not a young man anymore. No longer that young, gritty

Green Beret who led mission after bloody mission, maneuvering through the jungles of Vietnam and other places he could not mention. He must now be content with what he was and who he was becoming. His future days, which had been many, were becoming fewer, and with the formal engagement of his two oldest daughters to fine young men, the reality of middle age had set in.

He thought he had accepted all of that. But the new sheriff had knocked him off balance. Sam was accustomed to being called out by the county sheriff to lend his capabilities when the down and dirty was needed to help track a fugitive or locate a missing child. He was the accepted expert in the woods for the real tough stuff, and he had garnered quite a reputation with the department. But this new man had no regard for him, as the Scriptures so pithily expressed — *another king arose, which knew not Joseph.* The new sheriff had the confidence of his own youth, with new ideas and others he chose to rely upon. That was his privilege and prerogative.

And perhaps he was right — maybe Sam wasn't so special after all.

That was all right, Sam told himself. It was all right if he had been put on the shelf, if he wasn't needed anymore. Even old Green Berets must eventually retire. He decided that he would forever put away his tiger fatigues and never wear them again. They had been a symbol to remind him of who he was, a person he was no longer. His day had come and gone. He would make himself content with managing the farm, and if he had to, he would let others do the heavier lifting. Perhaps now he might be able to spend more time with his beloved Mary, hope for grandchildren to spoil, and find solace at the end of the day in his easy chair.

Sam paused at the river's edge to allow his horse to drink. The hollow was dark and sometimes forbidding if you did not know it well. As Sam looked up the river, he realized that less than a mile or so upstream, a young teenage boy was lost, hungry, and frightened. He wished the sheriff and his men Godspeed to find him. He would have liked to have helped, but the most important thing after all was that Billy be found safe and well.

Seven

A Farmer's Life

It was very early morning and still dark on the big farm. Everyone was in their beds except for Brenda, who was alone in the kitchen, rolling out a pan of biscuits and slicing up a bowl of potatoes for frying. Hastily tidying up the counter and shaking out her apron, she quickly slipped on her jacket and carried the food out to her car. Returning to lock the door, she met Mary standing on the top step of the porch.

"Brenda, where are you going so early this morning?" she asked. Brenda looked down for a moment and then spoke. "Ma, I didn't mean to slink around behind your back, but with all the grief about Billy, I didn't want to add to it with my problems. Joe's mother is sick, and I was just helping out with meals. I didn't think you would mind."

"Brenda, you should have told us. Of course we don't mind. Has the doctor been there to see Maudie?"

"Dr. Cumberland was there, but he just said she's old and worn out and needs plenty of rest. I'm trying to help out the best way I can."

"I don't want you wearing yourself out so you can't finish school," Mary said seriously.

"Joe needs me, Ma. He works so hard, and I thought with Maudie sick, it would be nice for him to have some good hot food to look forward to."

"Honey, we can all help out. You don't have to bear this all by yourself." Mary reached out and brushed some flour from her daughter's cheek. "Grandma Andrews and the girls will be glad to pitch in."

"I appreciate that, Ma, but I must do this by myself. I'll be all right. I promise."

Mary smiled. "Okay, dear. I think I understand. Let us know if it gets to be too much. We all need a hand eventually. I hope Joe appreciates the rare gem he's getting for a wife."

* * *

As she approached the Schenkle farm, Brenda could see the kitchen light ablaze and a light shining in the barn. *This is a farmer's life,* she thought. *Up every day before the sun.*

Joe would certainly be at his chores by now and famished by breakfast time. Hurrying up the steps into the kitchen, she could see the sink piled with dishes from yesterday. The strong smell of bitter old coffee was coming from the pot on the stove. Evidently, Joe had just added water to the cold pot of dark liquid from last night and reheated it.

Brenda smiled at Joe's mess and went into Maudie's bedroom to check on her. She was awake and smiled when she saw Brenda.

"How are you feeling this morning, Mrs. Schenkle? Can I get you something?" Brenda said, kissing her on the cheek.

Maudie reached her arms out to Brenda to pull her close. "Oh, it's good to see you, dear. I suppose the place looks like a tornado came for a visit. Sorry for that."

Brenda pulled a chair up to the bed. "Don't worry about a thing, Mrs. Schenkle. I'll tidy it up as soon as I get breakfast on. Do you feel like a bite this morning?"

"Maybe a biscuit and some coffee if you don't mind," Maudie answered. "And dear, would you please do me the favor of calling me Ma? 'Mrs. Schenkle' makes me feel like a stranger."

"Okay—Ma. Just lay back and rest. Holler if you need anything," Brenda said as she pushed the chair up to the wall again and walked back to the kitchen.

Brenda turned the oven on and lit the pilot light with a match from the dispenser on the wall. There was a momentary rush of gas and then a loud "woof" as the blue flames flared up. Brenda set the temperature for biscuits and then lit the burners, starting a pot of fresh coffee, and put the potatoes and bacon on to fry. She ran some hot soapy water into the dishpan in the sink and set the dirty dishes to soak.

As the potatoes and bacon began to crisp, Brenda removed the foil from the tray of fresh-cut biscuits and slid it into the oven. Soon they would be golden brown and ready to drip with butter. She debated whether or not to make a pan of country gravy to go with the biscuits. It certainly was no trick to make a quick pan of gravy.

But Joe might want something later on, she thought. *Gravy and biscuits would be just the ticket.*

The sun finally broke through the trees as Brenda stepped onto the porch to call Joe to breakfast. The air was cool and fresh, and she could hear roosters crowing to each other from the four corners of the Shanghai neighborhood. Grasping the braided leather strap to the dinner bell mounted on a pole next to the steps, she shook it back and forth, the familiar clang and clatter breaking the morning silence. After several minutes, Brenda could see Joe coming from the barn with a small pail of milk and a basket of fresh eggs. She stepped down to meet him, kissing him and giving him a hug.

He smiled sheepishly. "Sorry, Brenda, about the messy house and all. With Ma sick, it kinda got away from me. I wish I had some brothers and sisters to help out. I think after I was born, the folks got a look at me and lost courage."

Brenda chuckled. "Aww, and I'll bet you were a cute little baby too. I enjoy helping out and cooking, Joe." She winked. "I'm going to be doing a lot of that for you pretty soon."

"Thanks for being so understanding, Brenda. How is Ma doing?" Joe asked as Brenda took the basket of eggs from his hand.

"Doing fine, I think. I made her a little breakfast, and she seems to be feeling better. Later I'm going to see if she wants to sit up in a chair for a while. Is Dr. Cumberland coming to see her?"

"Yes, he said he would come by around noon. Maybe we can invite him to dinner—would that be okay with you?" Joe asked.

"I think that would be a great idea. I'm going to put a chicken on to stew and roll out some noodles to go with it. Mashed potatoes, chicken gravy, creamed wax beans, and maybe a rhubarb pie if I have time." They went into the kitchen together, and Brenda gave Joe a friendly shove. "Now wash up and sit down to breakfast before the biscuits get cold."

Eight
The Sheriff Calls It Off

That evening after the supper dishes were put away, the Bridges sat together in the living room, mostly trying not to think about Billy. Feeling helpless apart from their prayers, they all wondered what could have happened to a young man in supposedly civilized Berrien County. Friends in the department had been keeping them updated, but word so far had not been good. Lien especially was taking it hard. She sat in the corner, pale and silent.

Shattering the silence, the phone rang. It was Chief Jorgans calling to tell Sam that the search for Billy Gussette had been called off. The sheriff had found evidence that Billy had been in the woods but was unable to locate him. Believing that he and his men had left no stone unturned, he was convinced the young man was no longer there. Without any further news or hard information like an actual physical sighting, the sheriff had declared that further effort was futile.

Rookie! Sam thought with disgust. *So—because you can't find the boy, that means he's not there and we stop looking!*

Chief Jorgans had been standing there when the new sheriff humiliated Sam by glibly dismissing him as a relic.

Now, as police chief of Sodus, Jorgans would be left alone to pick up the pieces and explain to Mrs. Gussette why they had not found her boy. He vowed that even if he had to bow and scrape, he would implore Sam to take up the search and do what he could on his own. "I'm asking you, Sam, as a friend," Chief Jorgans said.

"Chief, I'll do whatever I can," Sam said. Hanging up the phone, he paused for a moment in thought, his hand still on the receiver. He then turned to Lien, who was standing silently behind him.

"Lien, do you know anything about Billy Gussette's intentions to go into the woods off River Road?"

Lien jumped like she'd been hit by a lightning bolt and looked up into Sam's eyes, beginning to squirm. She had been growing up fast, but now, before her father, she was just a little girl again.

Sam eyed his daughter. Her obvious discomfort with his question told him she knew something. He silently motioned for her to take a seat at the kitchen table. "What do you know about it?"

Lien looked pitifully up at Sam and slowly began to relate the things Billy had told her—about his mother losing her job, the Indian cemetery, and a chance to earn some quick money by selling a valuable Indian carving. "Daddy, Billy asked me not to tell and made me promise. I shouldn't have done it, but he begged me. I wanted to tell you about it several times, but I just couldn't go back on my word."

Sam stared at his daughter and then spoke, his heart heavy with the possibilities. Anger flared as he realized that Lien could have prevented all of this. "Lien, do you realize that Billy's mother is sitting at home right now heartsick, not knowing if he's alive or dead? The sheriff and his men have spent many hours searching for him without success. You knew about this debacle and said nothing? There are some promises you should never make, and this was one of them. If I had known, I might have been able to intervene and do something about it. Now I have to try to find him myself—if he's still alive!"

Mary, who was standing at the doorway to the kitchen, pulled out a chair and sat next to Lien, who was fighting back tears. This was the first time Sam had spoken to her this way, and she seemed to be desperately seeking a sword to fall upon. He could see how his words had impacted her, but the stakes were too high to try to make amends now.

"Mary, I'm going to get some of my gear together. Would you make me a couple of sandwiches and a thermos of black coffee? It's going to be a long night." Even as he spoke, he began pulling things out of the closet by the kitchen door and then headed upstairs to his room to change clothes.

Sam was ready in less than a half-hour, and he paused to pick up the paper sack and thermos bottle from the corner of the table. "I'll be back when I can, Mary," he said, pecking her on the cheek. "Tell Karl he's going to have to hold down the fort. You and the girls pray for me, okay?"

Mary watched Sam as he turned to the kitchen door, surprised to see him dressed in blue jeans and a brown cotton duck jacket. His web gear and knife was the only vestige of his days in the military. She shivered when she thought about him in those dark, frightening woods all night by himself, but she also knew that he would be in his element. He often preferred to work alone anyway. With the Lord's help, Sam would be in control, not the circumstances.

Sam opened the door to leave but then paused, looking back at his daughter, whose silent tears filled her eyes. Pulling the door shut again, he walked back to where she sat and tenderly kissed and hugged her, speaking a few personal words to her in Vietnamese. Then leaving again, he closed the door and disappeared into the chill and darkness of the evening air.

* * *

As the dull red rim of the sun broke the horizon in a clear sky, Sam sat on a tree stump at the edge of the woods on the hill and closed the valve of his gas lantern. Taking a final sip of putrid black coffee that had long grown thick and cold, he took a bite out of his last sandwich and shoved it back into the paper sack. It had been a long night.

Poor Boy's Woods indeed! What a horrible place for a kid to be lost! Sam wondered about the noble-hearted but foolish boy who was willing to risk his life for a few paltry dollars to help his poor mother. If only he had known Billy's circumstances earlier!

Sam could hear a car coming down the road, and he watched as it parked next to his pickup truck. It was the Sodus Township squad car, and Chief Jorgans got out, holding a thermos of fresh coffee and a sack of warm doughnuts. "Hey Sam," he said, walking over. "I was hoping you'd be here. Thought you could use some fresh coffee and a sugar fix!"

"Thanks, Chief. It's been a long, weary night," Sam said, grateful for something sweet to eat and a friendly face.

"I spoke to the sheriff this morning, and he's not in a very good mood. I think he's a little embarrassed after the things he said to you the other day. When he and his men were out here, the dogs picked up the boy's scent just fine but spent their time crisscrossing the river bottom down there without success. Billy had definitely been here, but they just couldn't find him. The men found a feed sack and spade, but the boy's tracks led back out to the river and that's all. The water at that point is not deep enough to drown a flea. I don't know!" The chief threw up his hands in frustration. "How about you, Sam—see anything?"

"I was looking for anything that shouldn't be there—scraps of paper, torn clothing, broken twigs—but nothing," Sam answered. "I tried to locate the Indian cemetery, but it was nowhere to be found, if it even still exists. It's as though the ground just swallowed Billy up."

The two men sipped their coffees, deep in thought, silently munching the still warm doughnuts. "Chief?" Sam asked, breaking the silence. "Did the sheriff say anything else?"

The chief hesitated and kicked at a pinecone. "Come on, Chief," Sam said with a sideways look. "I can take it."

"Well, he made a comment about you wearing your old army uniform. He says you have a problem with 'moving on' and 'letting go of the past.' He referred to you as an anachronism— whatever that is."

"Oh, he said that, did he?" Sam said with a big grin. "Well, perhaps he's right, but you won't be seeing that uniform anymore. I've decided to hang it up for good because—"

"Sam?" the chief interrupted. "You don't have to explain yourself to me. I'm sorry I imposed upon you to come out here in the first place. This is a younger man's game, and well, I'm sure that with all that's happened, you have your farm to run and a family to care for."

Sam smiled. "Not you too, Chief?" he said, chuckling. "Between you and the sheriff, I'm thinking I should be in a nursing home."

"Now I didn't mean that at all, Sam. We both do what we can at our particular slice of life, and I think the sheriff was out of line. He'll find out soon enough what it's like, by golly! Any other man would have been offended and refused to come back out here after that. I'm just saying that you've given more than your share over the years, and we all appreciate it."

"Well, I'm not saying I'm not offended," Sam said, smiling as he poured the dregs of his old coffee to the ground, "but being offended doesn't find Billy. Chief, there's an old legend about this place, about how it got its name and such. I'm sure you're familiar with it."

"I am—sort of bizarre, isn't it?"

"That it is. But maybe there's a link between Billy's disappearance and the legend. We must consider that."

The chief tossed his cup into the front seat of his squad car. "You don't mean a supernatural explanation, do you?"

"No, but if you look hard enough, you may find a germ of truth even in old legends," Sam countered.

"This boy's father and I were good friends," the chief said thoughtfully. "I remember the day he was shot. He was a fine deputy, and I could have been a better friend to his widow and son. I wish we could find him, Sam—alive if we can." Despair crept into the chief's voice. "I know you're into this kind of stuff. If this was the jungle, what would a guy like you do?"

"Chief, one of the old sergeants who mentored me told me that anytime I started believing the books and movies and hype about the Green Berets, I should just take off my shirt and see if there was a letter 'S' tattooed on my chest for 'Superman.' If I didn't find it there, I was to remember I'm just a man without superpowers. The best man is just a man at best, as they say, but what I do have is some training and experience. Between us we have covered almost every acre of this forest, and with dogs to boot, and we still haven't found the boy. My training has taught me how to function in a wilderness setting, but my experience—and frankly, a hunch—tells me not to be too quick to quit, to keep searching for that one thing we may have missed and haven't considered."

"But Sam, what do you think we could have missed?" the chief inquired, leaning back against the door of his squad car.

Sam sat quietly for a moment, thoughtful. "Years ago in 'Nam, an old friend of mine—Tom Biscotti, or 'Biscuit,' we used to call him—told me a story I will never forget. Tom was a chopper pilot in the Air Cav mostly flying Hueys in support of ground troops. A lot of the guys owed their skins to him—myself included. This crazy guy would fly his chopper anywhere under the worst conditions and heavy gunfire to pull soldiers out of harm's way. Once when my

Special Forces team was about to be overrun, Biscuit came out of nowhere and got us out. I remember he took a .50 caliber round right through the windshield just inches from his face. What an amazing man he was, and we loved him.

"The story I want to tell you, however, took place long before Vietnam, when Biscuit was a young man back in Texas just learning to fly. He had volunteered to take some medicine to a small hospital way off in the boondocks somewhere. The plane he was flying was an old two-seater crop duster and probably should have been in the scrapyard. Well, he was doing fine until the plane encountered a thick area of fog and he had to rely on his instruments to fly. Tom was a clever boy, and even at his young age, he was able to fly with instruments. Now, instruments are a fine thing to have on an aircraft as long as they work. But as Tom guided his plane along in the thick weather, he had a gut feeling that he was not level, that he might be flying too far sideways. He looked down at his attitude indicator, the thing that tells you your position relative to the horizon, and a chill ran up his spine. It wasn't working! He began pounding and banging frantically on the dash, but nothing. What was he going to do? Resign himself to the circumstances and just keep going until he crashed? No sir! Not Tom! He was a cowboy from the Big Bend country of Texas, and his pa had taught him to survive and think on his feet. He reached down in his pocket and took out a big chaw of tobacco, and when he had his saliva glands working really well, he let some of the brown juice dribble out of his mouth. If the plane was flying straight and level, Tom figured, gravity should cause the tobacco juice to run straight down his chin—but it didn't. It streaked out the side of his mouth and into his left ear. He was banking hard on his left. Tom slowly adjusted the plane's controls until the juice ran down the center of his chin, telling him he was level again. *As long as the tobacco and my spit holds out*, Tom told himself, *I might be able to keep this plane flying straight until I get out of this fog.*"

Sam smiled at the open-mouthed trout expression on the police chief's face. "Tom used that same bravery and horse sense in Vietnam. Some said he was reckless, but I don't agree. Men sometimes put limits on themselves and then try to put those same limits on others. I contend that there are always options open for the right man. Biscuit was one of those men."

Sam straightened his shoulders. "So, Chief, what I'm trying to say is that when you come to the end of your rope, consider that there might be another possibility, another way out. All of the evidence says Billy is gone, but my gut tells me he should still be here. Let's consider that and work with that for now — for his sake and his mother's. If Billy is dead, there is nothing more we can do for him. But if he *is* still here and alive, we must further consider the places we haven't searched. Now, the weather is moderate and very dry. A healthy young sprout should be able to survive for a while if not injured too badly."

"What are you talking about, Sam? What other places? We've searched everywhere!"

Sam shook his head slowly and stood. "Chief Jorgans, I don't mean to sound so mysterious, but I'm going home to take a shower and recharge my batteries with a few hours of sleep; then I'll go back out."

"Sam, do you want me to go with you this time?"

"No, Chief. I'll go it alone and let you know as soon as I learn something—either way." He started his pickup truck and waved good-bye.

Sam soon arrived at the big house and immediately headed upstairs.

"Mary, I'm going for a shower and a few hours of sleep. Wake me so I don't sleep past noon. I have to resume the search as soon as possible." Sam gave his wife a tender kiss. "I'd appreciate it if you could pack some more food and coffee for me to take along and fill my canteen with hot tea and plenty of honey. Throw a couple of those chocolate bars you bought the other day in my bag too. I'll need to keep my strength up, and I predict it's going to be a long day—and possibly an even longer night. And Mary, would you ask Brenda to go to the Sodus Library for me this morning and ask to borrow any old plat books and terrain maps they may have of the township—the older the better? See you in a few." As Mary nodded, bewildered, Sam trudged up the steep stairway of the old farmhouse to bed.

Nine
Seeking Comfort— Finding Fault

It was noon when Sam returned to the woods to continue looking for Billy. Lien lay on her bed with an afghan pulled up around her shoulders. She had already harvested a box of tissues, which were strewn at random across her bed and floor, and had started on another. Finally, her supply of tears nearly exhausted, she couldn't lie there anymore. The fact that poor Billy seemed hopelessly lost, unable to be found despite all the effort that had been expended looking for him, could not be remedied with weeping. Now her dear Sam was out there, weary and worn, having taken up the search in those horrible woods by himself. He might be injured and Billy might be dead, and there had been a moment in time when she possessed the power to intervene. How could she ever have agreed to keep silent about such a thing? Had she convinced herself that somehow Billy was capable of pulling it off? But if he had, what about the taking of Indian artifacts from a grave and deceiving his mother? Everything about this fiasco was wrong, and she had let it happen, and now she might never see him again!

Lien knew she had a lot to answer for, and she didn't know where to start in sorting it out. Billy had done this thing on his own, she understood that, but she had to bear some of the responsibility for standing by and doing nothing.

Rising from her bed, she splashed her face with cold water and ran a brush through her hair. *Perhaps one of the girls is here,* she thought as she walked down the hallway to the room her sisters shared. Peeking around the corner, she could see Amberley in her familiar place at her blue wicker desk, working on a paper for school. Lien silently walked in and sat on the edge of the bed, waiting for an opportune moment to speak.

"There," Amberley said out loud, closing her notebook and turning around in her chair, coming almost face-to-face with her little sister. "Lien!" Amberley cried out, holding her hand against her heart. "Sweetie, you've got to stop being so quiet! You're like a cat! At least tap on the door or something."

"Sorry, sis," Lien responded, expressionless. "I didn't mean to surprise you. Do you have time to talk?"

Without waiting for an answer, Lien began to unload all of her thoughts and feelings on Amberley as the waterworks started again. "It's tearing me apart! What if Dad can't find Billy? How can I bear what I've done?"

Amberley fought back her own tears. Holding out her arms, she spoke softly. "Come here, honey," she said, holding Lien tightly. "Lien, it's true you shouldn't have agreed to keep this quiet, but we don't know what else was on Billy's mind. I'm sure he would have gone anyway, even if you had refused to keep his secret. If someone is bound to do something they will do it, so stop taking the blame for something that's really not your fault. Besides, Billy thinks the world of you. I'm sure if you had refused to keep his secret, he would have realized you did it because you care for him. You told him how you felt and tried to talk him out of it. Billy made his own decision, and he must in the end bear the responsibility for himself."

"But what about Dad?" Lien exclaimed. "He was so very angry with me! He hates me!"

Amberley smiled and smoothed back her sister's hair. "Now stop it! Dad doesn't hate you, and you know it. He was just responding to the situation like a father. You know how he is. He loves you very much, and when this is all over, he will come and speak with you about it. I promise."

Amberley held Lien until she finally spoke. "Thanks Amber. I feel so much better. I was hurting so much inside that I was having trouble breathing. You are a good sister."

Kissing Lien's forehead, Amberley smiled and stood up. "And so are you. I wish there was a way we could all stay together always and not go our separate ways. That is the bitter sweetness of growing up. But I will always—"

Amberley didn't finish the sentence. Her face went blank, and she collapsed on the floor, barely catching the side of the bed with her arms.

Lien froze in horror. "Amber!" she cried out.

Amberley held the edge of the bed as if it were the side of a rocky cliff. "Lien, help me onto the bed!"

Summoning all of her strength, Lien was able to get her sister off the floor. Amber laid her head back on her pillow, her eyes rolling at the ceiling as she breathed heavily. "Why can't I get well? Hank is surely going to get rid of me!" she moaned, mostly to herself.

Lien made a quick dash to the bedroom door. "Let me get Ma!" she said.

"Please Lien, don't tell Ma. There's nothing she can do. There's nothing anyone can do. Hank will leave me, and I will be all alone. Nothing anyone can do." Amberley repeated the words over and over until her weeping made her voice unintelligible.

Lien paused for a moment and then called down the stairs to Mary. She was done keeping secrets that didn't help anybody. Mary made haste and came up the stairs, taking a seat next to her daughter. Cooling Amberley's face with a damp washcloth, she turned to Lien. "Call Dr. Cumberland; tell him . . . tell him that it's more of the same!"

Ten
No More Time to Spare

It was well past midnight when a weary Sam Bridges walked up the steps to the kitchen door, dropping his muddy gear on the porch behind him. He was glad to have made it back to the house, for he could hear the distant rumbling of a thunderstorm making its way across Lake Michigan. Ambling over to the sink, he washed his hands and splashed water on his face. It felt good and cleared his head a little. The house was quiet, and everyone was in bed. Mary had left him a covered plate of warm food on the stove, and the coffee was still hot.

Sam had picked up the fallen mantle of the sheriff's department, perhaps with a little pride in his heart to show the arrogant sheriff he still had what it takes, but alas, he had done no better than they. Poor Billy Gussette was still missing.

Sam remembered a similar search several years ago in Hipps Hollow when they had discovered their now adopted daughter, Lien, sleeping on a bed of straw. But Billy seemed gone for good. Even the dogs had eventually lost interest in searching for him, failing to alert on a trail grown cold. Now would come the tears, the broken hearts and the suffering of loss. Billy's mother had already experienced her share of sorrow, and now her only son was gone, without even a body to claim and gaze upon one final time. Sam's heart was heavy with grief. Billy had never known his father. Perhaps if he had, he might have enjoyed a father's love and counsel that would have kept him from taking such a foolish risk.

Sam picked up his plate of food and coffee, and carrying it into the living room, he snapped on the lamp and sat down in his favorite chair. After taking a few bites and a sip, he picked up his Bible from the table and opened it to the third chapter of the book of Proverbs. Sam read two of his favorite verses and considered them:

Trust in the LORD with all thine heart; and lean not unto thine own understanding. In all thy ways acknowledge him, and he shall direct thy paths.

Resolve set in again. Sam was exhausted, running on fumes and desperately in need of sleep, but he had to be sure he had done everything possible to find poor Billy Gussette. The thunder from the distance was getting closer, and he could hear the rising wind stirring the trees outside the house. Quickly finishing his food, he set the empty plate on the table next to him. His intention was to rest his eyes for a few moments and then mount the stairs to bed, but the invisible mist of uncontrolled weariness took charge, and Sam's unshaven chin slowly sank against his breastbone.

Sam awoke with a shudder as a nearby lightning strike and explosion of thunder resonated through the house. For a brief moment he was back in the war, and he could smell the acrid smoke from fired artillery rounds. Scratching his itchy hair and beard, he cleared his throat and took one last gulp of cold coffee. *It sure dies hard,* he thought to himself.

Picking up his plate and cup, he plodded into the kitchen and set them in the sink. Reaching over to turn off the light switch, he noticed several books and papers setting on the corner of the table. They were the old plat books and topography maps of Sodus Township that he had asked Brenda to borrow from the library. Sam glanced over at the stairway leading to a hot shower and his bed, then with resignation, he gathered up the stack of materials and made his way back into the living room to his chair. There was no point in going out to search again until the storm died off.

Turning on the lamp once more, he noticed an old newspaper article on top of the pile preserved in a yellowing acetate sleeve. He began to read:

THE LEGEND
OF POOR BOY'S WOODS

Scattered among the fields and roadways of rural Berrien County are countless, lonely patches of forest and woods, cloaking the meandering rutted scars of primitive pioneer roads and long forgotten paths of forest Indians. Some are now mere hedgerows of sumac, Osage orange, black willows and the occasional crab apple tree or wild plum, populating the ditches and fence lines of the countryside. Still others are isolated islands of trees, surrounded by oceans of grain and seasonal crops, neglected and ignored by the farmer because the land is difficult and refuses to suffer the plow. A few of the larger fragments of woods still linger, growing on the hilly, uneven ground along rivers, creeks and gullies—ever unfit for cultivation and difficult to trek. One of these particular settings straddles the shoreline of the St. Joseph River along the lonely River Road in Sodus Township. A remnant of the native forest that once covered the lower peninsula of Michigan near the popular resort know as Tabor Farm, this place was to become the venue for a chilling, little known account that would mark it as infamous for many years.

Evidently, a country boy whose name is long forgotten, living on his father's farm in southern Sodus Township, was walking home one lazy autumn afternoon from one of the several one-roomed schoolhouses that peppered the township in those days. Skipping in play along a rough, dusty portion of River Road, he discovered that his favorite arrowhead, a cherished gift from his father, was lost through a hole in his pocket. The young lad, being overcome with a terrible fit of grief, attempted to retrace his steps to discover it but to no avail. Wiping his tears and bidding good-bye to a school chum he had enlisted to help him in his search, the boy decided to take the rugged path through the "forbidden" woods along the river in hopes of procuring another stone point from an Indian family who lived there amidst an oak opening. *Maybe*, he thought, *a little Indian boy might trade me an arrowhead for an apple or the shiny new nail giv'd to me by the blacksmith in town.*

Whatever did happen is not known, for the little boy never returned home and was soon reported missing by his parents. School was closed and local farmers left their toils and shopkeepers closed their shutters to search the thick expanse of woods, but the lad was never seen or heard from again. Some say he drowned in the river or sank in the grips of the quicksand muck and mire common in that area. Others speculated that he was kidnapped by the Indians and secreted away to some remote tribe in upper Michigan or Ontario. Supernatural explanations were offered, but nothing could dry the tears or ease the sorrow of his grieving folks. Mothers for many years thereafter would ring their hands and shake their heads, exclaiming "Poor boy!" whenever the tragedy was mentioned.

Since that day, children have been admonished to walk straight home after school and warned to eschew the river and the dark halls of "Poor Boy's Woods," and only the very brave or very foolish dare go near it. And as no farmer wishes to possess it, the tax rolls ever carry it as abandoned property. So long ago was the incident that no official documentation survives to substantiate it. The tale lives on only in the subtle telling, mostly kept alive by old men and farmers smoking their pipes, seated around blazing woodstoves in the teeth of wintertime gloom—a ghost story to be told to children around smoky October bonfires.

Sam rubbed his jaw, noting the flowery writing style of the old article. Opening the fragile book of maps, with its musty smell and old cover that left rust-red smudges on his fingers, he took his magnifying glass out of the drawer next to his chair. Thumbing through the brittle, yellowed pages, he located a rough, hand-drawn map of the woods showing the topography between the river and the road as it appeared back then. The map was almost a century old, but even so, Sam recognized much of the terrain, having been intimate with it the last few days. As he traced along the riverbank with his finger, he noticed a series of small circles he had never encountered on a map before. Scanning the map's legend at the bottom of the page, he found that the circles were sinkholes.

"Sinkholes!" Sam said under his breath, surprised. *Who would have thought? I know there are naturally occurring sinkholes in Michigan, but I hadn't heard of any in Sodus Township.* Then he remembered the remark he had flippantly made to the chief concerning Billy—*it's as though the ground just swallowed him up.*

Sinkholes were places where soft rock and soil had washed or dissolved away from harder rock layers underground. Sometimes they appeared as mere holes in the earth, but some became deep pockets or caves that could easily conceal a young boy if he fell into one. And since it had been dry all summer and had not rained for weeks, the river's water level would have certainly dropped and exposed some of these old sinkholes—if they still existed.

Sam's eyes grew larger as he suddenly realized that though it had been dry in Michigan, it had been raining for several days along the northern border of Indiana, especially across the large city of South Bend. South Bend got its unusual name for being the "south bend" of the St. Joseph River, which placed it miles upstream from Sodus. Surely, the river must be rising from the rain as it flowed north from Indiana through Sodus to empty into Lake Michigan. And with a storm brewing across the big lake, the sluice gates in the Berrien Springs dam would be opened to release the mounting water pressure in the river, causing any existing sinkholes along the Sodus shore to soon fill up with water. There was indeed no more time to spare.

Feeling his soul wither inside from fatigue, Sam thought of Billy out there, perhaps trapped and terrified in a hole in the ground, rapidly filling with rain and rising river water. He had to find his second wind.

Taking the wrinkled, muddy map of the woods he had been using for the last few days, Sam quickly noted the approximate locations of the sinkholes in pencil. Then he quickly scribbled a note to Mary and left it on the table against the sugar bowl. The farm still needed tending, but fortunately, Brenda was capable of doing the milking in a pinch, and perhaps Joe and Lien could help as well.

Sam paused on his way out the door. He couldn't do this alone. He was desperately in need of someone he could trust, someone with special skills. He was fortunate to have that someone living under his roof, and while he was loath to do so, he knocked on the door to Karl and Beth's room off the corner of the kitchen and waited. Soon, a sleepy Karl stood there, smoothing his hair back with his hand. "Sam? What is it?"

"Hey, Ranger," Sam said with a grim smile. "Sorry to wake you, but I need your help."

Eleven
Finding Grace

Amberley sat up in bed in the darkness of her room as the pattering rain on the roof above stirred her from a deep sleep. She was sure she had heard voices downstairs but figured it must have been a dream, or perhaps part of the embarrassing spell she had suffered the evening before. Ma and Lien had been so tender and caring, staying with her until she fell asleep. She looked over at Brenda, who was resting soundly in the bed next to hers; she did not remember her coming in. Amberley smiled to herself, comforted in thinking how much her family loved her and was there for her, as always.

Doctor Cumberland wanted her to have some tests done as soon as possible. It was inevitable that Hank would find out. Amberley had wanted to keep her recurring illness to herself, hoping it would go away, but it had come back as present and familiar as an old friend. While in contemplation, and perhaps mixed with a bit of self-pity, she had realized that all along, she'd wanted God to heal her instead of praying that He would have His way. She wanted Him to make her physically whole, but instead, He was sending His grace. Amberley was finally coming to understand that her illness was her lot from the Lord, and because of that, she could live with it.

* * *

Sam hastily replenished his bag of sandwiches and coffee as Karl readied himself, and soon the pickup was bumping and sliding along the muddy ruts and gravel of the long driveway as Sam breathed out a prayer for wisdom. As Sam and Karl neared their destination, they noticed there were no streetlamps burning or lights from distant houses shining through the trees. Apparently, the electricity in this corner of Sodus Township had gone out due to the storm, making the woods and fields along River Road as dark as pitch, only momentarily illuminated by random flashes of lightning.

And as Sam and Karl peered over the edge of the ravine into Poor Boy's Woods, the rain fell heavier about them into that cauldron of seething black ink. The men quickly took their bearings, and tying a long rope to a stout tree, they began working their way down the steep, slippery sides to the forest floor below. They held out their lanterns in front of them, the darkness soaking up the light like a sponge filling with water.

Sam stopped near the edge of the river. As he'd feared, the water was noticeably rising. He quickly located several tall, straight saplings, and he cut them close to the ground and stripped off their leaves and branches with his hatchet. Handing one to Karl he said, "Use this to poke and prod around for any holes, and be sure of your footing. We don't need any broken bones." Then, taking off his hat and holding the lantern high in the air as the rain struck his face, he said thoughtfully, "Oh well, so much for the help of a full moon tonight."

The two old soldiers searched along the eastern bank of the river for about an hour with no results. There was no sign of a sinkhole, much less Billy. Sam set down his lantern and carefully rechecked the map. "We've searched all of the spots noted, Karl. I'm surprised we haven't located at least one of the holes. Who knows? After a hundred years they might have all been filled in."

Karl grunted his agreement as Sam folded the map. "I have to make sure for Billy's sake. The map didn't show any sinkholes further south, but that doesn't mean they're not there. Let's see what's down there." Sam gave his gas lantern a few more pumps to brighten the light. "I'll poke about close to the shore, and you can work the area further out," he said to Karl.

"This sort of reminds me of searching for Viet Cong hiding in their tunnels. It's hard to think I once crawled down into those creepy places with nothing but a flashlight and a forty-five," Karl said.

"I remember," Sam responded. "Not one of my favorite memories of that place."

Another half-hour passed as Sam worked his way around the steadily rising water of the shoreline, trying to imagine what a sixteen-year-old boy would be thinking or doing in this situation. As he poked his stick through the heavy brush, the lantern light reflected off a piece of paper on the ground. Sam stooped to pick it up and held it near the light to examine it. There, scrawled in pencil on a folded page of school notebook paper, was an old assignment belonging to Billy.

The hair on his neck bristled as he began to breathe harder. Billy had been along this way! Sam smiled and stuffed the dripping paper in his pocket. Then he heard Karl stumble a few yards out from where he stood. "Whoa!" Karl shouted out. "Sam! This way!"

As the rain fell steadily, Sam spun on his heels to find Karl and felt something strike against his right leg just above his boot line. A sharp, tingling pain, like a wasp sting or salty sweat in an open wound, stabbed him. Sam lifted his lantern and caught the glimpse of a small, dark snake hanging from the cuff of his blue jeans. Quickly grabbing it, he slung it away into the invisible darkness of the flowing river. Pulling up his pants leg, he squatted down on a wet, mossy log and held the lantern close. There was only one bite hole with a trickle of blood, but it was unmistakable. Sam was sure he had been bitten by a massasauga rattler, a small species of rattlesnake and the only venomous snake indigenous to Michigan. This swampy, undisturbed woods was just what it liked when seeking places to hibernate for the winter. Sam had never seen one in the flesh, as they were normally shy and bit only if harassed or stepped upon. Well, it seemed he'd stepped on this one.

Sam felt his ankle for swelling but there was none, and the expected intense pain from the snake's venom did not come. His head remained clear, and after sitting for several minutes, he was sure that the short-fanged snake had given him a "dry bite." Rattlesnakes can control their venom and sometimes will bite for defense but not inject their poison. Pulling down his pants leg, Sam grasped the handle of his lantern and headed in Karl's direction, thankful and hoping that Billy had not met with one of these "narrow fellows in the grass," as the poet called them.

Sam quickly found Karl, who had been making repeated stabs at the brushy ground with his sapling pole when it slipped through his fingers, disappearing into a hidden hole. The sudden lack of resistance surprised him and caused him to buckle to his knees—the stumble Sam had heard.

Karl recovered his lantern and let out a loud whistle as Sam joined him. There before them was a deep hole about three feet across. Sam stooped to lower his lantern deep into the hole. "Billy? Billy Gussette? Are you in there, son? It's Mr. Bridges!" he shouted.

Sam listened intently, but there was only the sound of rain and rushing air through the dark shaft, causing his lantern to hiss like a startled cat. Sam shouted several more times, but there was no answer.

Sam took in their surroundings a little more carefully. The river was very close. "In a normal year of rainfall, this hole would be underwater. I'm not sure just how stable the ground is around the hole, but with all this rain and rising water, I want to avoid putting all of my weight on it. Let's cut a few more of these saplings, Karl, and build a tripod for support. I have a spool of paracord in my bag to use as lashing. It will spread out my weight away from the center of the hole, and then I can use it to drop straight down inside and hopefully find Billy." Karl nodded, and Sam went on. "I also brought along a piece of pipe and an old crank handle we might use to cobble together a primitive windlass for the rope, in case there's not enough room to shinny back up on my own."

Soon the frame was completed, and Sam unloosed the rope from around his shoulder and threaded one end through the pipe and handle at the top. Testing it with several strong tugs and satisfied that it could let him down through the hole and pull him back up again, he wrapped the other end of the rope around behind his bottom, holding it above with his left hand and below with his right.

Karl grabbed Sam by the arm. "Sam, let me go down there. I've done this sort of thing a whole lot and I'm younger—" Karl halted midsentence. "Sorry, Sam—didn't mean that."

"No offense taken, Karl, but because you are younger and stronger, I need you topside to pull me back out. Besides, if Billy is down there, he might be in shock and need to see a friendly face that he recognizes. He's never met you before. If and when I yank this rope, start pulling me up."

Sam slowly started his drop through the hole, being careful not to burn himself with the hot lantern tied in front of him. He controlled the speed of his descent by letting the rope slowly and carefully slide through his gloved hands.

The air got sharply cooler as Sam descended, and the sound of it rushing past him was like the low, steady moan of a winter's night. He spit out a mouthful of mud that fell loose from the side of the hole, ever mindful that it could cave in on him in an instant.

His boots touched bottom after about ten feet. Sam bounced up and down to test the ground, and satisfied that it would hold, he dropped to his knees. Untying the lantern from his belt, he looked around, preparing himself for whatever was down here.

He was surprised to discover that the narrow shaft opened up into a fairly large, cavern-like room. The stench of the place was vile, reeking of damp earth, dead fish, and dead animals: mold, rot, and decay. Letting his eyes focus, Sam scanned the cave carefully, noting that its floor was strewn with the bones and fur of animals that had fallen into the hole over the years when the water was low and were unable to get back out. He was painfully aware that the mud and rainwater from above were beginning to trickle down the sides of the long, dark shaft with ever-growing intensity. He was also aware that soon, the rising waters of the St. Joseph River would also be pouring in.

As Sam held his lantern high, his scalp prickled to see a pair of eyes shining back at him a distance away. Instantly reaching for the knife that hung from his shoulder strap, he tensed up, preparing for anything, but then loosened his grip and called out softly, "Billy? It's Mr. Bridges. Come here, son."

There, tucked tightly into a rocky crevice like a startled crawdad, was Billy Gussette. He did not speak, but when Sam reached out and called his name again, he crawled toward the light and placed his hand in Sam's, allowing Sam to pull him close.

Sam set the lantern down and held Billy tightly. The boy shivered as he held onto Sam with all his might, struggling to control himself. Sam massaged the muscles of Billy's arms and back to help his circulation.

"Hey there, buddy! How you feelin'? Are you ready to go home?"

Billy's dry voice crackled as he tried to answer.

"I'll bet those guys at school won't pick on you anymore. None of them would ever be brave enough to do what you just did. What do you think, Billy?"

Billy said nothing.

"That's right. You're one tough nut to crack. Lien would be so proud of you right now."

Billy looked up into Sam's face and tried to smile as a tear escaped his eye. Quickly wiping it away, he created a smear of mud on his cheek.

"There's no shame, Billy," Sam said. "I've shed a few tears myself over the years, and most of them as a grown man. Sometimes it's the only thing left to do that helps."

Sam unsnapped his canteen from his belt and unscrewed the top. "Here, son. Take a couple swigs from this. It's warm tea with honey in it."

Billy took the canteen and after several long gulps, began to cough.

"Not too fast, now—just sip it. There's more where that came from. And I'll bet you're hungry too!"

Sam reached into his pocket, pulling out a chocolate bar and peeling back the paper. "Here, young sir. This will make you feel better."

Billy took the candy bar from Sam and quickly gobbled it down. This, with Sam's kind words and presence, put a sparkle of hope in his eyes.

"There, are we ready to go home?" Sam asked, brushing the tangled, matted hair out of Billy's face.

"Yes sir," Billy finally answered, his voice hoarse. He rubbed his eyes.

"Let's go then," Sam said. "I'll bet you could eat a whole cow right now. How would you like, say, some fried eggs, bacon, hash-browned potatoes, and orange juice?"

"Yes, sir," Billy replied with a smile.

"And a tall stack of waffles with melting butter and hot maple syrup—would that help to blow away the cobwebs?"

Billy nodded his head. His eyes were filling with tears again, and this time he didn't rub them away.

"I'll bet Mrs. Bridges is making that for breakfast right now. So let's get out of here. I'm making myself hungry thinking about it."

Sam looped the end of the rope carefully under Billy's arms. "Karl is topside, Billy. You don't know Karl yet, but he's a swell guy. He was an Airborne Ranger in Vietnam, just like your papa." Sam took off his boonie hat and squashed it on Billy's head. "This will keep the mud out of your face."

With several yanks on the rope, Sam shouted up the long dirt shaft—"Pull 'er up, Karl!"

Swiftly, Billy was pulled to the surface. Karl brushed him off, wrapping him in a wool blanket. He then lowered the rope back down the hole, awaiting Sam's signal.

Sam took a few moments to look around the cavern with his lantern. Tucked in one of the corners among the many animal bones, he noticed something that caught his eye. As he crawled over to it, lifting his lantern, Sam sucked in a deep breath and froze.

After a few moments, he backed out again to the bottom of the shaft. "Karl!" he shouted. "Throw me that cloth feed sack we brought along—just toss it into the hole."

Sam grabbed the sack as it fell and returned to the place in the cavern, carefully placing the objects he'd found inside. Tying the sack to his belt, he gave the rope several yanks and was pulled to the surface by Karl.

Once on solid ground again, Sam tied a red handkerchief to the sapling frame as a marker. He would return when the water had again receded and place a steel grate over the hole so no other unwary boy could fall in.

"Test your legs, Billy, to see if they work," Karl said. Billy walked a few steps and then nodded to Karl. As they made their way back out of the dark woods, Sam turned and held his lantern high, noticing with a shiver that the rising water level was only a few yards from Billy's sinkhole.

Sam ascended the hill first to help Karl, who was carrying Billy on his shoulders. Soon, muddy and tired, they were all safely in the warm pickup truck, headed back to Hipps Hollow.

Twelve
Two Boys Go Home

It was still dark and raining when Sam and Karl entered the back door to the kitchen. Mary, Grandma Andrews, and Beth were up, busily making breakfast. Brenda and Lien had already started the milking, and Joe was on his way over to help.

"Mary, look who I have here," Sam shouted, removing his muddy boots and dropping his web gear outside the kitchen door.

Mary turned to look, sliding a hot iron skillet from the burner. "Oh, it's Billy! Billy is here," she said, rushing over to give him a hug. "Sam! You found him!"

With his arm around the boy, Sam said, "Mary, I promised Billy here a fine breakfast of bacon and eggs, fried potatoes, and waffles. Do you think we can accommodate him?"

"Would pancakes do just as well?" Mary asked.

"'Won't do, Mary! I promised him waffles with butter and maple syrup. You wouldn't want me to go back on my word? Now let's heat up the waffle iron," Sam said, pretending to fuss and scold. He turned to look at the boy again. "Billy? Let's run you upstairs for a good scrubbing before breakfast. I'm sure I have something you can wear."

As soon as Billy was upstairs in the tub, Sam motioned for Karl to speak with him on the porch. As soon as they exited, he handed over the pickup keys. "Here are my keys, Karl. Go get Mrs. Gussette in the village—you know where she lives. I'll call her and tell her you're coming."

Karl quietly left as Sam made his way into the living room to use the phone. After giving Mrs. Gussette the good news, he dialed the number to update the police chief.

Billy soon came down the stairs, lost in one of Sam's shirts and pants, much cleaner and feeling better than he had for several days. Lien sat next to Billy at the kitchen table and smiled at him. Her heart was light once more as she reached out to put her hand on top of his. "Billy, I am so happy you're all right. I will never agree to anything again that will hurt you," she said. "Promise me you will never ask me to do that."

Billy looked into her eyes. "Never," he said. "Your pa already talked to me and said that part of growing up is learning not to do foolish things. Boy, did I blow that one. Sorry to make all this trouble for everybody."

* * *

Later that morning after Billy was safely at home with his mother and Sam had a chance to clean up, he walked down the hallway to Amberley's room. Sitting on the edge of the bed, he looked at his daughter, who had been napping. She was flushed and leaning weakly against her pillows.

"Hey, sweetie. I hear you've not been feeling well," Sam said, taking her hand and leaning over to kiss her on the cheek.

Amberley looked up at her father as the tears began to well up in her eyes. "Oh, Daddy! I'm sick again!" she said, hugging his neck. "If Hank doesn't want me, can I live here with you and Ma always?"

Sam understood Amberley's nagging doubts about Hank and her health. "Now aren't we talking silly? Hank is very much in love with you. God brought you two together; accept that and stop crawfishing and making yourself miserable. That's just the same as doubting God. Now, do you feel like getting up and eating something? I'll send Lien up to help you get dressed, and then I'll take you to your place on the porch. The rain has stopped, and it's turning into a beautiful day." Sam stood up. "You know we found Billy and he's all right? There's a lot to be thankful for, Amber. Always remember that."

He walked to the doorway and stopped to smile and wink at his daughter. "Give a holler down the stairs when you're ready, and I'll come back up to give you a hand."

* * *

Later that evening after supper and a few hours of badly needed sleep, Sam slipped on his hat and jacket and made his way to the workshop by the barn. Unlocking the door and clicking on the light, he looked toward the rear of the long room at a rack of different lengths of drying lumber. Selecting a nice long board of beautiful yellow pine, he quickly measured it and cut it to size. Then with a chisel, the old carpenter installed brass hinges and a hasp to complete and assemble a small box with a tight-fitting lid.

Sam glanced over to the corner of the workshop floor where a large steamer trunk sat, very old and worn. It was all that remained of the earthly possessions of Jeb Sanders, the faithful hired hand who had worked for them for so many years and had passed away just before last Christmas. Sam paused for a moment and then kneeled down in front of the trunk to open the lid. Other than a few old clothes, Jeb's wallet and watch and some trinkets, there wasn't much to show for almost seventy years of life.

Spying something in brown paper and tied with white string, Sam picked it up and carefully unwrapped it. There inside was a sky-blue flannel blanket, carefully folded and tied together with a length of blue ribbon. Sam smiled. He remembered Jeb showing it to him once. It was the receiving blanket that had belonged to his son, who died shortly after his birth many years ago.

Sam let the trunk lid slam shut as he set the blanket on the workbench. Reaching into his pocket and retrieving a key, he unlocked a large drawer under the workbench and carefully withdrew a muddy feed sack. Sam carefully removed and assembled the contents on a clean sheet of white canvas. There, lying before him with a few buttons and bits of tattered old clothing, were the objects he had found and retrieved from Billy's sinkhole in Poor Boy's Woods—the complete skeleton of a young boy. Sam picked up the blue baby blanket and fitted it inside the wooden box with care, letting out a long sigh. Then giving his head a quick shake, he placed the boy's remains inside with it, locking it with a brass lock.

It's time to call for the chief, Sam thought. *I'll leave it to him to report it to the sheriff.*

* * *

Several weeks had passed, and on a soft autumn evening, Sam and Mary were in the kitchen alone. Supper was over, and Mary gazed out the kitchen window as she finished the last of the dishes. It was one of those rare times on the big farm when everyone seemed to be gone and the couple had the house to themselves. But it would not be an occasion to hold hands or casually chat on the porch swing with a cup of tea.

"He's here," Mary said soberly.

Sam set his cup down and opened the back door of the kitchen as a squad car came to a stop across from the porch. Sam noticed there were two men inside. He was expecting Chief Jorgans of the Sodus Township Police, but who was the other man?

He was surprised when he recognized the young sheriff who had treated him so cavalierly at their first meeting. Sam nodded at the chief as he opened the back door to his car. There on the seat was the small pine box Sam had made.

Sam said nothing but stood silently with his hands on his hips. The young sheriff smiled and offered his hand to Sam, who stared at it as if it were a red-hot horseshoe.

"I don't blame you for not wanting to take my hand, Mr. Bridges. I was pretty rough on you last time we met. I'm sorry, and I ask your pardon. I've always been a cocky sort and usually live to regret it. The chief here gave me quite a dressing-down for the way I treated you, and a few of the guys at the department took me to task too. And of course, I received a call from old Sheriff Warner. I was wrong about you and would like to offer you my friendship, but I understand if you don't want it."

Sam looked hard into the sheriff's face and then reached out to shake his hand. "It's water under the bridge, Sheriff."

The young sheriff smiled and nodded. "It's all set, Mr. Bridges," he said, pointing to the yellow pine box. "The remains have been formally released to you for burial. The coroner believes they are at least seventy-five to a hundred years old. Cause of death unknown. This little boy, whoever he was, might very well be the one from the old Sodus legend."

Sam reached in and pulled the box forward to himself. "It's as I suspected, Sheriff," he said, lifting the lid to view the contents. Chief Jorgans gave him an inquiring look. "I just want to make sure Jeb's blanket is still in here," Sam said. "And I needed one last look. Thank you, Sheriff and Chief, for all you've done."

Then Sam reached into his pocket and pulled out a small arrowhead from his collection and placed it in the box. "His father gave him his first one," Sam said. "He set great store by it, and it cost him so much." Then pausing again and taking a deep breath, Sam reached inside his jacket and pulled out his old green beret from his days with the Fifth Group in Vietnam. Looking at it hard, he fingered the yellow flash with its three red diagonal lines and its black-and-silver pin. Then tenderly, he placed it like a pillow under the little boy's skull. "Now," Sam whispered. "Let a Green Beret watch over you as you sleep, little man!"

The young sheriff and old chief brushed a tear from their eyes. "Are you sure you want to do that, Sam? It has to mean a lot to you," the chief said, placing his hand on Sam's shoulder.

"I always planned to give it to my son anyhow," Sam muttered. "This little boy deserves more than just to be tossed alone into a hole in the ground. He needs the honor much more than I need a shadow from my past."

Sam picked up the wooden box and carried it to the porch, placing it securely inside a larger metal box that he had made ready. Kneeling down beside it, Sam fastened a shiny new brass padlock to the hasp and squeezed it until it clicked.

"Sleep on, son," Sam said under his breath as he stood up and threw the key as far as he could across the yard. "No more gawking at you—not by anyone!"

The chief was thoughtful. "Sam, I was thinking. What a shame he doesn't have a name."

"I've already tended to that, Chief," Sam said, picking up the box. "Come and see, both of you."

The chief and the sheriff followed Sam as he trudged up the long orchard hill carrying the unassuming container in his arms. Mary followed close behind, carrying a pot of yellow chrysanthemums.

At the top of the hill, Sam set the metal box containing the handmade casket in a prepared hole, and after a short prayer, he covered it with shovelfuls of earth. Smoothing the ground with a rake, he scattered a few handfuls of grass seed over the spot. Sam had already purchased a small granite headstone for the grave, and Mary set the flowerpot next to it.

"Lien will undoubtedly plant some flowers here next spring," she remarked. "It just seems fitting that of all the people in the world, this little boy should have come to us for rest."

Sam and Mary stood silently, gazing upon the sight before them. Mary let her hand slip softly into Sam's as she read aloud the inscription carved on the stone:

JOHN SAMUEL BRIDGES
ADOPTED SON OF SAM AND MARY BRIDGES
"His name is John. And they marvelled all."
Luke 1:63

Thirteen
Filling an Empty Place

As the alarm clock struck 4:30 in the morning, Sam quickly grabbed it before it could ring out. Carefully throwing back the covers, he dressed in the dark, and giving Mary a kiss on the cheek, closed the bedroom door behind him and walked quietly down the hall to Lien's room. Opening the door, Sam snapped on the light and instantly began to laugh out loud. There, seated in her bedroom chair, was Lien, all dressed in her fishing clothes with her rod and reel in one hand and her tackle box on her lap, grinning up at him.

"So, you think you're pretty smart," Sam said. "How long have you been awake?"

Lien stood up. "About an hour, I think. I was too excited to sleep."

"Well, let's get going then. I was thinking of breakfast in Berrien Springs, and then we can meet the captain below the dam about six. He said the walleyes are biting like crazy."

Sam and Lien descended the stairs, and together they carried the lunch hamper that Mary had packed for them, along with all of their gear and equipment, out to the pickup truck. As they made their way down the long driveway to

Hipps Hollow Road, Sam looked over at his daughter, who had not stopped smiling. This was going to be their day together, doing the favorite thing they loved to do—fishing! The affairs of the last few weeks with Billy Gussette and Poor Boy's Woods had caused a shadow to fall across their relationship. Sam figured that spending some special time with Lien would go far in healing any real or imagined rift between them. He had chartered a boat to spend the day fishing in the St. Joseph River for walleye and catfish. Lien loved to fish, perhaps something garnered from her childhood days living in a fishing village in Vietnam.

Sam and Lien had breakfast in the small diner at the top of the hill near the bridge. They both had chopped steak and fried potatoes, scrambled eggs, and biscuits and gravy. It was a hearty Michigan breakfast, not as good as Ma's but fair. Soon they would meet the captain on his riverboat and spend most of the day trying to outdo each other by catching the biggest fish in the river.

Sam had planned to take some time during the day to speak with Lien, to explain why he had been upset with her, to assure her of his continued love . . . but it was unnecessary. She understood and was content. All was healed and forgotten, and whether they were racing across the snow-covered fields along Hillandale Road in a sleigh, enjoying a quiet buggy ride through the hollow on a rainy afternoon, riding to town in the pickup truck to purchase supplies, or just working around the farm together, Lien enjoyed being with her Sam more than anything.

He spoke to her in Vietnamese as they drove to the river, and she nestled closer to him. She was always moved when he spoke with her in the tongue of her birth. It was his secret pledge to her that he loved her, that he accepted her as she was, and that he did not want her to forget her past, and Lien loved him for it.

* * *

It had been several weeks since Billy's ordeal, and Sam had been thinking a lot about it. He also thought of the little boy he had buried on the orchard hill and how close Billy had come to the same end. Sam had always longed for a son to teach and rear up into a man. He and Mary didn't speak of it often, but they had stillborn twin boys in heaven who would have been younger brothers to Amberley. Their tiny little bodies had been put in a small white box and buried on top of Grandpa Andrews's grave. They were not able to have any more children after that, but the Lord had seen fit to give them two wonderful adopted daughters instead. Still, the desire for a son remained. Perhaps he could be more of a father to Billy and make an investment in his life.

The next day during late afternoon, Sam was driving through Sodus and decided to pull up into the alley next to the family's old house across from the railroad tracks and the coal yard. He shut off the engine of his pickup truck and sat still for a moment. There was the house that his family had occupied for so many years, part of them while he was fighting in Vietnam. He had trusted Christ as His Savior in that old house, and his life had been salvaged there. It was empty now, and as far as he knew had never been rented again after his family left.

Across the way was the house that had belonged to Mr. Enkins, his old boss, dear neighbor, and friend. Now he and his wife were gone, moved to Florida, and all was quiet. Sam looked down further. There was the house where Sharon Gussette and her son lived. She had never remarried after being widowed, and she struggled to make a living and rear her son. Hoping to find her at home, Sam got out of his truck and knocked on her door.

"Why, Mr. Bridges!" Mrs. Gussette said. "Please come in."

Sam took off his hat and sat at the kitchen table. The room was very small, but not much different from the kitchen in their old house. Accepting a cup of tea from Mrs. Gussette, he laid his hat on his lap.

"Ma'am, I just thought I would come by to check on Billy. How's he doing?"

"Oh, he is doing quite well. He sprang right back and seems to be more fascinated with his rescue than anything else. He is writing a story about it for school. He's kind of an army buff anyway and is so proud to have been rescued by a real Green Beret and an Airborne Ranger like his father," she answered.

Sam smiled. "He'll be okay then, tough little guy that he is. And how are you doing? Are you still working at the hospital?"

Her face brightened. "I was working as a receptionist at Berrien General, but my job was eliminated—downsizing, you know. We were having a tough time of it. Dr. Cumberland heard what had happened and spoke up for me. I was hired in another department, and it looks like it will be a pretty stable situation."

"Good old Doc Cumberland! Happy for you, ma'am," Sam said, taking a sip from his cup. "But I had another reason for stopping by. Do you think Billy would mind spending some time on our farm? I was thinking he could come over and work with Karl and me on Saturdays for a few hours. It would give him a chance to learn some things and pal around with some guys. It might also help him vent away any mischievous energy."

Mrs. Gussette clasped her hands together. "Oh, Mr. Bridges! Would you? I have so wanted Billy to be able to do something like that. I just know he would be thrilled to work with you and Mr. McNee."

Sam stood up. "It's a deal, then. You clear it with Billy, and I'll have Karl pick him up in time for breakfast this Saturday. I'll pay him a dollar per hour to start if that's agreeable, and we'll work out the details as we go along." Sam tipped his hat. "I know we'll enjoy having him over."

"Oh no, Mr. Bridges, you needn't pay him. He would be glad to work just for the experience and camaraderie."

Sam smiled. "I'll pay him so he can learn that a good man gets paid for his efforts. 'Arbeit macht das Leben suss,' as the old German saying goes: 'Work makes life sweet,' especially when it's sweetened with pay well earned."

* * *

Early the next Saturday morning after the milking, Karl drove over to Sodus to pick up Billy. The boy quickly ran out to the truck as Karl pulled up and closed the door behind him.

"Hello, Billy," Karl said. "I see you're ready to go this morning."

"Yes sir, Mr. McNee. I've been up since five o'clock."

Karl laughed. "Firstly, you may call me Karl. We're going to work together and undoubtedly become pals, so we must be on a first-name basis. And if I'd known you were such an early riser, I would have shown you how we milk cows. Maybe next week." He nudged Billy with his elbow.

Karl was soon turning down the long driveway to the farm. He parked opposite the big porch. "I thought we'd have breakfast first and then we can gather the eggs. How does that sound?"

"Great, Mr. McNee . . . I mean Karl."

Breakfast was cheerful. Billy held up his head as he sat between Karl and Sam, clearly feeling grown-up now that he had a real job. Lien winked at him from her place across the table.

Billy beamed back at her. He didn't think life could get any better. Just a few days ago he was headed down disaster's path, almost to a tragic end. Now he felt like somebody. He was beginning to sense how important his time with Karl and Sam would be, or as much as a sixteen-year-old boy could.

Karl introduced him to a pretty young woman at the table. "Billy, this is Mrs. McNee, my wife. She was a nurse in Vietnam where I first met her. She could sure tell you some wild stories."

Billy, not sure of what to do, reached out and shook her hand. She smiled at this young man trying to get his manners right. "Billy, you can call me Beth, and if you ever have any questions, just ask."

90

Billy quickly learned to gather the eggs without upsetting the hens too much. Karl was an endless source of teaching. "Billy, you notice that we have the nests away from the roosts, which are positioned higher and further back. This discourages the hens from sleeping over their nests and makes it so you don't have to walk through the droppings to gather the eggs. Also, you get fewer soiled eggs that way. Now let's take them over to the egg-washing station."

Karl and Billy carried the wire baskets of eggs into a room in the corner of the henhouse. "We need to wash and sanitize the eggs before we pack them into cartons. Be sure to wash your hands well when you're done. Chickens and eggs taste good, but they can carry certain diseases that we don't want to spread."

Billy was fascinated by it all and felt that he wanted to be a farmer someday, though he also wanted to be a sheriff's deputy and an army Ranger like his dad. His head was spinning, and almost as soon as he started working, it was time for lunch. "Let's eat first, Billy, and then I will take you home," Karl said.

After lunch, Billy gathered his things to leave. "Here you go," Sam said, handing him an envelope. He carefully opened it. Inside were four one-dollar bills and four quarters. Billy looked up at Sam in amazement. He had never earned five dollars at one time before.

"Before you go, Billy, take a seat and let's have a chat," Sam said.

Billy nodded and followed Sam outside. Sitting together on the top step of the porch, Sam looked directly into Billy's eyes. "Billy, a boy needs to learn how to work when he's young so he will be worth something when he becomes a man. Let me give you a Bible verse to chew on: 'It is good for a man that he bear the yoke in his youth.' Many young boys these days just while away the days and the hours, wasting their time, and when they become men, they can't hold down a job because they have never been taught to work. Don't let that happen to you."

Sam folded his arms across his chest and continued, "I know that when you're young and earning money for the first time, the urge is there to blow it all on something. I want you to learn how to manage your money. Will you let me teach you a few things?"

Billy nodded. He'd been in awe of Sam since the rescue and was glad to learn from him.

"Now, you have five dollars. Ten percent of that, right off the top, should go into the offering plate at church. Do you understand that?"

"Yes, sir. Ten percent would be fifty cents," Billy answered.

Sam smiled. "Very good, Billy. You calculate rapidly. Ten percent is called a tithe in the Bible, and that goes to God. We give it, not because we must, but because we love Him and want to do it. Besides, God's people should support God's work. Remember, Billy, how you spend your money usually shows what is important to you in life and the condition of your heart."

Billy nodded again, concentrating as Sam continued. "Now, we don't want to be stingy with God since He is not stingy with us, so let's give Him a little more. Everything we give above the ten percent or tithe is called an offering. So let's give another twenty-five cents. Is that agreeable?"

"Yes, sir," Billy answered.

"And remember, Billy: God gets the first fruits before you spend one dime on yourself, so don't make Him stand in line with all the bill collectors. Next," Sam said, "you should put some of this away. How about next week I pick you up and take you to the bank in Sodus and we open up a savings account for you? The bank will give you a bankbook, and each time you deposit money with them, they will write it down for you. If you do this each and every week, the amount will grow and the bank will pay you interest for keeping your money with them. Does that sound like something you would like to do?"

Billy nodded his head. "Thank you, Mr. Bridges. I would like that very much."

"Okay, Billy. Now talk it over with your mother and get her approval. I'll see you in a few days," Sam said, patting him on the back.

* * *

For the next several Saturdays, Karl picked up Billy early in the morning to spend a few hours on the big farm in Hipps Hollow. Billy relished it more and more and dreaded it when the time came for him to go back home. He often wondered how it would have been if his father had lived, and he was thankful for Karl and Sam's efforts to fill that empty place in his life. He knew they were doing it on purpose, just because they cared.

On one particular Saturday afternoon after lunch, as Karl drove him back to his home down the alley in Sodus, Billy spoke thoughtfully. "Karl, when I fell into that big hole in the ground, I was so scared. I froze and couldn't move. I called out for help, but nobody came. It was so dark and smelly, and the wind just howled. I kept thinkin' that something was gonna jump out at me from the dark—was I a coward?"

Karl didn't seem surprised that Billy was still thinking about Poor Boy's Woods. "No, Billy, you were not a coward. Your reaction to what happened was normal. You've never been taught what to do in a situation like that. Full-grown men would have acted the same way, and most of them wouldn't have handled it as well as you did. But I will say this, you kept your head screwed on straight, and I'm proud of you for that."

"But how could I have gotten out of that hole by myself?"

Karl looked at Billy soberly. "You probably couldn't have, Billy. Sometimes we get into situations where escape is not possible. The only way you could have gotten out of that hole by yourself was to never have fallen into it in the first place. It was a very foolish thing you did, going off like that. I understand why you did it, but you almost destroyed your mother with grief and sorrow."

Billy hung his head. Karl's voice grew gentler. "All right, son, no more of that. You feel bad enough without me hitting you over the head with it."

Billy was silent for a few moments but finally spoke. "I know I did wrong, but I saw it as a chance to help my mother. Karl, could you teach me how not to be afraid in the woods—like a Ranger?"

Karl pulled up into the alley in front of Billy's house, pausing to tap his fingers on the steering wheel. "Let me talk it over with Sam. I have some ideas, and if your mother doesn't mind, we'll see what we can do."

Billy pulled on the door handle to leave when Karl spoke. "See you next week, Billy."

Quickly shaking hands with Karl, he slammed the door behind him and hurried into his humble house.

* * *

Several days later at the breakfast table, the milk truck from the dairy having already departed, Karl decided to confide in Sam about his conversation with Billy. Sam said nothing but listened over a bowl of grits that steamed up his new glasses—another subtle reminder that time was marching on.

"Karl?" Sam finally said after some thought. "I think we've been missing the boat. I've an idea, and I want to know what you think. Billy has been coming over every Saturday morning to work for a few hours, so instead of taking him right home after lunch, how about we set aside an hour or so to start teaching him some survival techniques and woodsman's lore? We can work with him through the winter, perhaps until the spring, and then we can suggest that we form a club. I would prefer to do this through our church, if possible, as a ministry. Let's gather our ideas together and have a talk with Pastor Mitchell. Billy can recruit some of the boys from school, especially the ones who have been giving him a hard time. We can start teaching them the same things we are teaching Billy. He will be pretty far advanced by then and can help us teach. That will give him some credibility among the guys, and perhaps we can be a positive influence on them as well. I can speak with the sheriff, and I'm sure he would provide some people to come out and speak with the boys now and then. What do you think?"

Karl took a bite out of his toast. "I think it's a great idea, Sam. Perhaps Billy would not have gotten into trouble in the first place if he had known a few things. How do you want to begin?"

Sam took a sip from his cup and gazed out the window across the fields. "Winter will be here soon, so let's hold off on camping for now until he learns some things and gains some confidence. We need to toughen him up a bit first. Let's start by showing him how to put together a survival kit—you know, a fire starter, first-aid kit, and a fishing kit— and then we can go from there."

"Sounds good," Karl said. "I'm sure we can help some of these kids. But most of all, let's do it for Billy's father."

Fourteen
Dr. Cumberland's Dream

Hank sat at the table in the staff lounge of the hospital, weary to the bone and scribbling away to catch up on his paperwork. Dr. Cumberland, his mentor of several years, sauntered into the lounge after doing his rounds, his bamboo cane hanging from the crook of his arm. Pouring coffee into his old stained cup and taking a cookie off the plate on the counter, the old medico sat down and smiled at Hank. Hank glanced up at him, nodded, and smiled back as he kept scribbling. He was looking forward to taking a short nap in the old leather recliner in the corner as soon as he finished.

"Did you ever wonder," Dr. Cumberland began, pouring some of his coffee into a saucer to cool, "how much more work we could get done as doctors if we didn't have to write so much? Nobody understands what we write anyway, or so they tell us."

Hank smiled at the humor, perceiving a change and easiness in Dr. Cumberland's voice and manner. Sort of the way you sense you are growing up the first time your father speaks to you as an adult and not a child.

Dr. Cumberland took a bite of his cookie and continued to chat on various subjects until Hank began to squirm in his seat. He didn't want to appear irritated or disrespectful, but he had a stack of reports to finish, and that big chair in the corner was calling out to him.

The old doctor ate the last crumbs of his confection and lifted the saucer to his lips to take a sip. Hank felt the doctor's eyes on him and reached his finger into his collar to loosen it. Why Dr. Cumberland had chosen this particular time to be chatty Hank did not know, but it was obvious he wanted to talk.

Hank finally put down his pen and sat back in his chair. "What is it, Doc? Something on your mind?"

Cumberland smiled and paused for several moments. "I know your father set you up with several offers from some mighty prestigious hospitals. You are a bright doctor, Hank, and could have your pick of any plum. Your time with me and this hospital is about over, and well, I wondered if you had made a decision."

Hank picked up his pen from the table again and began tapping it thoughtfully against the sugar bowl. "Doc, no matter how hard I try, I can't find anything that thrills me. It seems that everyone knows what I should be doing but me."

Cumberland cleared his throat. "Excuse the forthrightness, but have you discussed this with Amber? I think she might be able to render you some sound advice."

Hank tossed his pen on the table. "I think I'm making her a little crazy because I haven't made a decision. She thinks I'm purposely keeping her in the dark and dragging my feet. Well, maybe I am. I don't want to agree to a wedding date until I'm sure and settled."

Cumberland smiled and gave his head a quick shake. "Why do young people think they have to do this and that before they get married? You could marry her now and then take your time deciding what 'thrills' you. Think about how happy it would make Amber if you came home to her regular, to a nice supper and a loving family." His expression grew more serious, and he wagged a finger at Hank. "Mind you, her physical maladies will probably be with her always, and that means with *you* always. Is that going to be a problem?"

Hank sat up straight and looked seriously at Dr. Cumberland. "Not a bit of it! My feelings for Amberley are love—not pity. I couldn't do without her."

Cumberland leaned forward. "And have you told her this? I don't mean the usual vaporings of lovers in love, but have you squeezed her hand and let her know that her illness doesn't matter one wit to you, that you belong to each other until death puts an end to it? I won't mince my words, son. Amberley needs to know that she is more important to you than your career. Keeping her guessing about her future and her wedding day is going to put her out of kilter. It borders on the cruel. And has it occurred to you that what thrills you should also thrill your wife?"

Hank looked hard at Dr. Cumberland, surprised at his candor. "Did Amber put you up to this?"

"No, no . . . I arrived at all my conclusions by myself. It's just that I'm old and ornery, and bold enough to speak my mind without caring much about what people might think."

Dr. Cumberland laid his cane across his lap. "Let me tell you something and I'm through. I was a young doctor once and had a dream that I wanted to see to fruition before hearing any wedding bells. I made a lovely girl wait and wait until she married another man. I ended up an old country sawbones with no wife to love me and see me through the rough spots of life. I was also left with an unfulfilled dream, set adrift with no one with whom I could share it. I lost both ways. Don't spend your life in the valley of decision, Hank, only to eventually find yourself alone and miserable."

"What was your dream, Doc?" Hank asked.

Cumberland stood up, his baggy suit draped around his bony frame. "I might tell you someday, Dr. Wheeler, if you and Amber ever get things straightened out. Don't waste the springtime of your life, son. Soon the summer will be here with all its heat, humidity, and biting bugs, and then you will slowly lose heart, forcing yourself to settle for what comes."

Dr. Cumberland opened the door to depart, and as he turned his head to look back at the weary young resident, he saw himself more vividly than ever before. "Good night, Dr. Wheeler," he said, switching off the light and allowing the door to close on the darkened room.

Hank smiled at the bizarre conversation, and leaning back in his chair, he closed his eyes.

Fifteen
Maudie Goes Home

Brenda slowly turned into Joe's driveway, the damp gravel crackling and crunching under the tires of her Studebaker. She turned off the engine and listened. The farm was silent and still, without even the sound of a hen clucking or a rooster crowing. Careful not to slam the car door, she noticed the dismal gray sky and low hanging clouds as she walked up onto the porch. Knocking twice, she entered, and there at the kitchen table sat Joe. He looked up at her with mild surprise, saying nothing for several moments as the wall clock ticked in her ear. Pulling out a chair from the table and moving it next to him, she sat down and leaned over, resting her head against his shoulder.

"I guess I'm really all alone now," Joe finally said. "Bowerman from the funeral parlor came last evening to get Ma. It's . . . it's so quiet in here today."

Brenda slowly interlaced the fingers of her left hand in Joe's, squeezing them firmly. "You look so tired. Let me make you a hot breakfast, and then I'll help you with the chores. The animals don't seem to take notice of the affairs of men, do they? They want attention whether it's a holiday, a Sunday, or a day like today."

Brenda stood up and hung her jacket on the hook behind the door, then quickly busied herself at the stove. "I'll have coffee ready in about ten minutes. Why don't you see about running a razor across that face of yours? You look terrible," she said with a gentle smile. Joe nodded and mechanically walked into the other room.

Soon, Brenda set a plate of scrambled eggs and American fried potatoes, a bowl of grits, and several golden brown biscuits covered in a cloth on the table at Joe's place and poured him a steaming cup of black coffee. "Come and eat, Joe. A farmer has to keep up his strength."

Joe sat down with his fresh face and combed hair. "This looks good. I like the way you make eggs," he said, breathing out a quick prayer of thanks and then picking up his fork.

Brenda joined him, breaking off half a biscuit and dabbing it with apricot jam. As Joe ate his breakfast, she looked at him. He was so weary, much too weary for a young man; the kind of weariness that gives gray hairs and wrinkles before one's time. His mother had been sickly the last few years of her life, and Joe had been the son of her old age, born when she was well into her forties. He had spent as much time looking after her as he did the farm, especially after his father's death.

Quickly clearing the table and washing the few dishes, she joined him outside, feeding the chickens and collecting the eggs. Joe fed the pigs and the cows, shoveled manure, and laid down fresh straw in the stalls. Brenda helped milk the few cows Joe owned, a time-consuming process as he did not have a modern milking system like that on her dad's farm. It had to be done the old-fashioned way with a stool and bucket, but she enjoyed working with him on his place with its sounds and smells. Soon the animals were content, and Joe and Brenda headed to the house to wash up.

"Joe?" Brenda said afterward as they sat on the porch swing together. "I am so sorry about Maudie. We are going to miss her, but she was so miserable. She's with your pa now, and that's a happy thought."

"I know. I must keep reminding myself of that. My days were kept full, taking care of her and the farm. Now it's just me, and that will take some getting used to. I'm not looking forward to being alone and lonely."

Brenda took Joe's hand and held it in both her hands, looking into his handsome face. "Joe, it doesn't have to be that way."

He looked into her smiling eyes, as shiny and brown as sorghum molasses. "What do you mean?" he asked, suddenly looking nervous.

"I mean we can get married now. My college and expenses are already paid for, and Amber gave me the Studebaker so I will have transportation. There is no reason for us not to be together."

Joe smiled but remained serious. "Brenda, I don't want to drag you into my world of drudgery and toil. You're too beautiful and smart for that. I don't want to see you get old before your time."

Brenda held him close and smiled. "Joe, did you just say 'drudgery and toil'?"

Joe nudged her with his elbow. "Stop it! Are you surprised? You taught me good English, after all."

She laughed. "Joe, I'm not a soap bubble lit out on a blade of grass—fragile and in need of constant protection. I am strong and able to help you. Marrying you is not a sacrifice. I love you and want to be your wife. And I'm not looking to have babies when I'm in my forties. I want to start a brood right now, when we're still young enough to enjoy them and have the energy to rear them up right."

Joe kissed her on the forehead. "What will your folks say?"

"I think they'll be happy for us. The idea of grandchildren has always appealed to my dad, and I can't imagine them not wanting us to get married."

"Then it's your lookout," Joe teased, "but isn't the man supposed to do the asking?"

"If I waited for you to get around to it, Joe, the question would never get asked." Brenda squeezed his hand. "But I want to tell Amber first before I tell anyone else. I owe it to her. Let's finish the rest of the chores, and then we can have supper at my place. Amber says she has a surprise for the family and wants everyone to be there."

* * *

Grandma Andrews plucked the last piece of golden-brown chicken from the sizzling oil and set it on the paper to drain. Then Brenda lifted the large platter and placed it at the center of the table. The nearby bowl of mashed potatoes steamed with melting butter like golden sunshine on top of a snow-covered mountain. Mary had made her green beans with sautéed onions, flavored with ham drippings. Lien put on her oven mittens and slid a long tray of sourdough dinner rolls from the oven. They were very special because they were made from Grandma's yeast sponge, which was over fifty years old. A pitcher of sweetened ice tea rounded out the meal as everyone gravitated to the table to enjoy the repast.

Amberley stood at the kitchen window, tapping her foot against the baseboard, upset and not really bothering to hide it. This day meant a lot to her, and she was looking forward to sharing the happy news with those closest to her. The entire family was seated and ready to eat, but the person she most wanted here was absent. Hank's chair was empty. He had promised to be here for dinner . . . but she had heard that promise before. In his defense, he was often at the mercy of the hospital, and she had known them to come and get him for some emergency before he could make it to the parking lot. He had not phoned, so that was likely what had happened. This had always been the pattern in their relationship, and she was forced to live with it. That didn't mean she was happy about it.

Amberley turned away from the window and watching the long driveway. She was disappointed but would not make the others wait.

After the cheerful meal, Amberley stood up and walked to the stairway, retrieving a stack of identical packages wrapped in gift paper. Placing one apiece in front of each person seated, including Hank's empty chair, she sat down again, bidding everyone to open their presents.

Lien was the first to tear the paper from her gift. "Amber! You did it. You wrote your first book!" she shouted. Soon everyone was holding their copy of

Amberley's first book, glossy and new. Lien read the title aloud, "*The Girl from Old Sodus* by Amberley Marion Bridges."

"Amber, I didn't know you had finished it, let alone found a publisher! I am so proud of you. This is what you always wanted," Mary said, rising to kiss her cheek. Brenda and Lien followed suit and gave their sister a long, congratulatory hug. "May this be the first of many," Brenda said.

Finally, Sam stood up and walked to Amberley's place and kissed her cheek. "We are all so happy and proud of you, Amber. I know how long you have agonized over this, and now it's reality. I will take my cup and repair to the living room to read it."

Amberley enjoyed her family's enthusiasm, but she was amazed at how quickly the glow of the moment began to wear off like a dying ember. She helped the others clear the table and wash the dishes, all the time looking out the kitchen window and up the long driveway for the missing automobile and the man who had not come.

Sixteen
Hank's Decision

The first few days in May marked the arrival of Baltimore orioles in their long, exhausting migration to Sodus Township. Traveling day and night, flocks of the weary birds seemed to suddenly appear at backyard feeders to gorge themselves on their favorite food—grape jelly. Seeking maple trees to build their hanging nests, the magnificent flashes of bright orange and black were pleasing to the soul and made even the hardest heart pause to appreciate them.

Amber took her place on the porch swing to watch the birds at Lien's feeder, wondering if her life would ever be well-ordered again. Everything seemed to go from turmoil to turmoil with just enough time in between to give the devil a chance to spit on his hands and start his goading all over again. When Hank asked her to marry him and his folks came for a visit on the Christmas before last, she was sure that all was well and it would only be a matter of setting a date. She had always envisioned a double wedding with Brenda, but now that was impossible. Joe and Brenda were married in a simple ceremony in the living room of the big house, and Amberley knew in her heart of hearts that there was no good reason for them to wait any longer. Their love for each other had matured and was ripe. Joe need not be alone anymore, and Brenda would be a lifelong tonic to the tenderhearted country bumpkin.

Amberley sat in the stillness of the moment, thinking about Hank. She had hoped that Brenda's wedding might inspire him, putting him in the "marrying mood," but he had said nothing to indicate that it had. Amberley missed being able to see him every day, and that only fueled her doubts and anxiety. He lived so close but seemed so far away.

Hank can be so frustrating! she thought to herself, and in her stubbornness she vowed not to mention the wedding again unless he did. If it was important enough, it would be up to him to prove it. Was this how it would always be, even if by some miracle they did get married? Perhaps she would be an old maid after all, living in this big house alone with a dozen cats.

Then, as was her way, she began to waver, thinking again of how Hank had stayed by her side when she was sick—always loving, always loyal. Perhaps the problem was with *her* and not with Hank. Was she just making him jump through hoops to prove himself again and again? Did she not trust him? Perhaps she didn't trust herself. How aggravated she felt!

* * *

Several days later in the early afternoon, Amberley and Lien were busy in the kitchen trussing up a young turkey for the oven. Hank was scheduled to finish his shift around three o'clock and hopefully would be coming for supper. He was exceptionally cheerful on the phone and told Amberley that he had news for her. Joe and Brenda would also be coming after finishing the late afternoon chores. Karl and Sam were out in the barn, and Mary had taken Beth and her little boy to see Dr. Cumberland.

The sisters spoke little among themselves as they prepared the supper, both anticipating and dreading Hank's news like an approaching thunderstorm, seeing the darkness on the far-off horizon, the flashes of lightning and the subtle stirring of the air. Hank, whose time as a resident here was almost done, was perhaps ready to finally level with his wife to be.

Lien also understood that a pattern of loneliness was about to begin in her life with Brenda gone, and soon, with Hank and Amberley's departure. Karl and Beth were living in Jeb's old room, but it was natural to assume they would one day build their own house and move away from the big farm. Lien was growing up quickly and would have to adjust to a quieter house with no sisters to tease her and help her with her girlhood troubles.

Amberley heard the sound of Hank's BMW in the driveway, much earlier than she had expected. Walking to the window, she peered out, quickly folding her apron and rushing out the door to meet him.

Hank slammed his car door and hurried up the steps. Putting his arms around her, he kissed her and sat down at the end of the porch swing, holding a long white cardboard cylinder under his arm. "Sit down, Amber. I have something to show you," he said, visibly excited.

Amberley smoothed her dress and sat down beside him. "What is it?" she asked with a breath of caution. Hank was cheerful and smiled. "I have some ideas and want to know what you think about them."

Amberley had waited for this moment for a long time, and now that it was here, she was struck with feelings of apprehension. Would she have to say good-bye to Sodus and follow her husband and be a doctor's wife, giving tea parties and dinners, forever uncomfortable around wealthy, sophisticated people who had no idea what it was to miss a meal because of poverty? *Maybe I'm being a snob?* she thought.

Amberley bit her bottom lip, waiting, hoping, looking into the smiling face of the man she had chosen to marry — that is, if he still wanted to marry her.

Seventeen
The Aging Warrior

The early morning chores were caught up, the milk truck from the dairy had come and gone, and Sam had asked Karl to supervise the plowing of a forty-acre section by some casual labor hired for the summer. The girls were off to school, and Mary, Grandma Andrews, and Beth had gone grocery shopping. Sam smiled as he turned on the stove to reheat the breakfast coffee pot. He would enjoy taking some precious moments alone with a fresh cup, a glazed doughnut, and yesterday's newspaper he had not yet read.

Just as Sam settled into his chair, the phone rang. He balked at the interruption and picked up the receiver. It was a voice he hadn't heard in years—Bill Adams, the former army captain and Green Beret who had resided in Washington for many years working for the State Department. It had been Adams and others who were responsible for rescuing Lien from being sent back to Vietnam many years ago. He had been a good friend and part of Sam's past . . . but why was he calling now?

"Sam, I wanted to find out how you're doing. It's been a few years. How is the little Vietnamese girl?"

"Hello, Bill. Everything is doing well here. Lien is just fine but not so little anymore. She is becoming quite a young lady. I would like her to meet you sometime."

"Perhaps I will, Sam. That was one of the most fulfilling missions I was ever a part of. It made me proud all over again to be in the Forces." He cleared his throat. "Listen, besides checking in on you and your daughter, I wanted to ask a favor."

Sam was curious. Bill knew all about Sam's past, but he also had to know that he was now only good for an occasional tramp through the woods to find a lost child. "Bill, I can't imagine what I could possibly do for you."

"Well, Sam, I just wanted to remind you how beautiful North Carolina is this time of year. How would you like to spend a couple of weeks' vacation there on Uncle Sam's tab?" Adams said with a chuckle.

Sam was quiet and hesitated. "North Carolina? You don't mean the Q Course?"

"I do. They are asking some of the old-timers to help out as an assistant cadre, and I thought of you."

"But Bill, have things gotten that bad that you have to dust off an old washed-up relic like me to help in a training exercise?" Sam said, his heart pounding in his chest.

The Special Forces Qualification Course, or Q Course, was a complex series of exercises where Special Forces candidates were trained and tested to put everything they had learned into practice under realistic conditions, namely, their combat and leadership skills. Candidates who successfully passed were awarded the coveted green beret. Sam's mind raced back to his time in the Q Course. It was grueling, and he was ever mindful that one slip up and he would be ejected and sent home. No one was more surprised and happier than he when he held his green beret in his hands for the first time. "Bill, what could I possibly do there? It's been years," Sam said. "How do you know I don't have a potbelly and a cane?"

"It's been the custom for years to use Special Forces veterans to help out during the Q Course. It's good for these young bucks to cast their eyes upon some of us old salts. And don't pretend you are washed up. I know what kind of shape you're in. When you rescued your daughter Brenda and located that missing boy when everyone else had given it up . . . what you did was brilliant and worthy of the Forces. Sam? I want you to do this, if not for me, for Sam Bridges."

Sam was surprised that Bill had kept tabs on him so closely throughout the years—that he knew not only about Lien but also about the rescue of Brenda from her abusive father and even his rescue of Billy Gussette.

"I'll send you the itinerary and anything else you might need. I'll also scare up another green beret with a Fifth Group flash to replace the one you buried with that little boy."

Sam was stunned. Apparently Bill had done his homework well. Just when he thought he would never wear his uniform again. "I'll do it, Bill. You don't know how much this means to me."

Adams's voice softened. "See you soon, Green Beret."

* * *

It was steamy warm and had been raining all day and far into the night. There was no moon, and except for the occasional lightning flash in the distance, the night was as dark as blackstrap molasses. Craig Willhausen was an excellent map reader and had aced every compass course he'd ever been on. He always checked and double-checked his coordinates before taking one step, so how he'd gotten off track, Craig was not sure. He had violated one of the axioms of the Special Forces—don't get lost.

Sitting down on a wet, mossy log next to a stream, he attempted to rectify his dilemma and get his bearings again. His compass was the only thing between him and endless wandering in the deep North Carolina woods.

Craig was in the middle of a Star Navigation exercise that had begun just after midnight, and several hours later, he suspected that he had plotted his coordinates incorrectly. But was he really lost? Many a deer hunter and soldier has discovered, to his embarrassment, that second-guessing one's compass can lead to disaster. Craig would trust his as gospel from now on and go ahead. He had no choice.

Something slithered across his combat boots and along the bank before him. Craig was startled and jumped back to a standing position. He had seen a large copperhead earlier that day, as big around as his forearm. He was not the nervous or jumpy type but was tired, and because something personal was bothering him, he had to struggle to keep his mind on what he was doing.

Craig had not seen or heard any of the other men making their way through the woods for hours, making him sure that he was hopelessly off his course. He felt his stomach growl and paused to take a bite out of a candy bar from his rations and wash it down with a gulp of water. The mosquitoes were bad, and he had already been bitten by a water bug as big as a fifty-cent piece. Looking at his watch, Craig wiped the sweat from his face on his shoulder and continued his trek through the sultry, dripping woods.

He had been so excited when he was accepted into the Special Forces X-ray Program. Although he was not prior military, this particular program was designed to attract exceptional talent from all walks of life, allowing him a shot at a Green Beret right off the streets. Craig was a PhD student of political science from a prestigious university, was fluent in German and Dutch thanks to his parents, and was in excellent physical condition. He was almost thirty, not married but engaged for some time. Carol was two years younger and had her PhD in economics. They had started out to be a typical "yuppie" couple and planned a teaching career together at the same university. Everything seemed smooth as silk until he decided to try out for the Special Forces. Carol had not been happy about it and was embarrassed to tell her anti-war, "progressive" friends. Several days ago her unhappiness had turned to contempt as she told Craig the wedding was off.

He tried to buck up and put the whole thing out of his mind, but there it was, pressing on him, urging him to quit and make up with her. A career in the Forces had been his dream, and he thought he had an above average chance of making it through. But now he was weeks into this particular phase of the qualification course and had seen too many men get dropped or quit. And for the first time, with Carol's ultimatum and "dear John" letter chewing into the back of his brain, the pressure and challenge of the Special Forces training and testing, and the miserable heat, darkness, and constant wet about him, his confidence was shaken. He felt his heart beating rapidly, and his breathing was hard. He had bragged to his buddies that he truly expected to go back home wearing a green beret, and now this.

Stumbling through the wet darkness, slipping on the pasty mud and tripping over hidden brush and thorny vines that seemed to reach out and snatch at his ankles, Craig stopped and leaned against a tree, his lungs heaving nervously for breath. Fear gripped his heart for the first time—not terror but the kind of fear that shakes you when you realize you are probably not going to make it. Fear that others will see you for what you are, that you have failed to carry the water and that they will be relieved that they are not you and don't have to work with you in combat when it really counts.

Craig's eyes started to water up, perhaps from the sting and burn of sweat or the insect repellant, or perhaps an emotional reaction to what was going on inside his head. He breathed hard and felt his chest flutter as he fought the reflex to panic. *Some Green Beret I would make!*

Then strangely in the distance he thought he could see a yellow light—little more than a glowing smear through the trees and brush. Another soldier?

Walking in the direction of the light, Craig decided that he was going to VW—voluntarily withdraw from the course. He would show Carol that he didn't need her, and in his convoluted thinking, he would punish her by punishing himself. With every footfall, he repeated in his mind, *I don't belong here!*

Cautiously approaching the light, Craig paused behind a large tree and watched. There in a small clearing stood a man with a flashlight. He was a point sitter, waiting to check him in and give him his new coordinates.

He wasn't lost after all.

"Come on in and let's chat," the man called out to Craig, beckoning with his hand. Craig tried to hide his surprise by loudly calling out his number and his point location.

"That's correct. Take a seat and fill your canteen while I get you your new coordinates," the man answered.

Craig observed the man, obviously a retired Green Beret from some other time and place, as he scribbled a few notes on a form. He was dressed in older style camouflage fatigues that Craig had only seen in photographs of the Vietnam War, with sergeant stripes on his collar and the distinctive arrowhead patch with the three lightning bolts on his left arm. On his head he wore a green beret with the colorful Fifth Group flash from the Vietnam era.

Putting down his notebook, the old sergeant looked into the face of the weary man who sat before him. "I'm Sergeant Sam Bridges, retired from Fifth Group."

Craig tried to smile. "Uh, Craig . . . Craig Willhausen."

"Did you think you were lost?" Bridges asked with a smile.

Craig opened his mouth, surprised, but no words came out.

"Well, Craig, your bearings are right on, and you are where you are supposed to be. And I'm glad to see you weren't following the road. That will get you kicked out of this course faster than anything."

Sam looked at the young man for a moment and then spoke. "Tell me, Craig. Why did you want to quit today?"

Craig's shoulders stiffened as he looked into Sam's face. "How did you know that, sir?"

Sam smiled. "I've seen that look too many times before, and I've seen it looking back at me in my own mirror a few times. What stumped you and made you want to throw in the towel?"

Craig glanced away into the distant blackness for a moment, slow to confide in the aging warrior.

"I thought . . . I thought I was lost out here because I missed one of my bearings. I struggled to pick it up again, and my confidence began to erode. My brain felt like it wanted to shut down. I was overcome with shame and realized I couldn't unleash that kind of guy on the Green Berets."

"What kind of guy? If you are here, there is something very special about you. I can tell by speaking with you that you are well educated, so you have proven that you know how to learn and therefore, we assume, are able to teach others. You speak at least one foreign language, maybe two, because I can detect an accent, so you have shown that you are equipped and willing to meet and interact with different people and cultures on their own level. You are in good physical shape, or you couldn't have made it this far. You're not afraid of the dark, so what is it? What flipped the switch in your head?"

Craig was hesitant, but he wanted to open his heart to someone, even this stranger who had obviously done it all

118

and won the prize, and who just might be able to steer him back on track. "I'm embarrassed to say . . . it's Carol, my fiancée. She couldn't abide me trying out for the Forces. She called me 'Tarzan' and said to come and see her when I was done swinging from the jungle vines. I didn't think it would bother me so much, but now it's eating at me. Her words really hurt, man, and now I'm thinking of quitting the course and patching things up with her."

Sam stood up and leaned his back against a tree, folding his arms. "That's what I would do, Craig, if that's what's important to you. I think you should patch things up and get married and have some kids. You have a degree, right? You should do all right financially in life, and then you can tell your sons someday about the time you almost became a Green Beret. And you will only wonder a thousand times through the years if you could have made it and what it would have been like."

Sam's words stung, and Craig hung his head.

"Look, Craig, I'm not a marriage counselor, and I don't know anything about your Carol. I'm sure she's a fine girl, but if she throws you over every time she doesn't agree with what you do, well, it's the tail wagging the dog. I could tell you stories about my life that would make you cry. I worked and prepared for what you're doing now more than anything I've ever done in my life. Once, I even had a root canal done by a dentist without Novocain to prove how tough I was. That's no joke! How many times I lost my way over the years, and while in 'Nam and Cambodia, I often wondered if I would ever see my wife and little girl again. The first war you have to win is the one with yourself. So your confidence took a kick in the pants and you lost it. Find out where you lost it, pick it up, and get going to the finish line. You learned a lesson about yourself today—you're not indestructible." Sam leaned forward and gripped Craig's hand firmly. "Nobody expects you to be. But if you want to wear that green beret, you'd better get the lead out. If you want to quit you can go back now, but perhaps, just perhaps, you are one of the few who can make it. If that's you, then let's move out!"

Craig nodded, but before he could step off, Sam stopped him. "Oh, and Craig, here is something that might help you," he said, reaching into his shirt pocket and retrieving an old black New Testament. "This was handed to me many years ago when I got on the bus in Detroit to head out for boot camp in Kentucky. I was just a boy then. I've been waiting to give it to someone who could use the help, and I guess that's you. I marked a few special verses that I'd like you to read. Let's just say it's helped me over the years to make me what I am."

Craig hesitated for a moment, stuffing the small book in his pocket and picking up his gear. Taking several steps, he turned to face Sam. "This is for you, Sarge," he said, raising his hand to his forehead in a sharp salute and quickly disappearing into the jungle-like woods of North Carolina.

Eighteen
It Has All Come Down to This

The little girl from Sodus who was born into poverty, who watched her family go through some of the darkest of days, who resigned herself to a lifetime of sickness, weakness, and uncertainty, stood in amazement in front of the long mirror in her room, enchanted by the glow of her wedding dress. Brenda and Lien stood next to her, struggling to fight back tears.

"I always did say you were the most beautiful, Amber, my 'goody-goody' little sister," Brenda said with quiver in her voice. "Now you are a princess, and in a few moments, you will finally have your prince."

"I won't be going far. My prince and I will be living here for a while until he finishes his time at the hospital," Amberley said, sniffing into a handkerchief.

"Sis, when are you going to tell us where you and Hank are going? Do we have to wake up some morning and find you gone?" Brenda asked seriously.

Amberley paused and then sat back on the edge of her bed. "Okay, I guess it doesn't matter any longer. You remember the day when Hank came to supper and brought with him a long, white cardboard cylinder? I couldn't imagine what it was. Opening it up and spreading it out on the table, I could see that it was an architect's drawing of a building and grounds. As you are well aware, Hank has been having a difficult time making a decision about his future—rather, our future. Between his parents, his friends and his sniveling fiancée putting pressure on him, he realized he wasn't making his decision according to what the Lord wanted him to do. After several conversations with Dr. Cumberland and a long season of prayer, something struck a chord with him. He had one of his father's architect friends in Chicago make up some drawings, and well, Hank wants to buy some land nearby and build a small medical school, specifically to provide training for doctors, nurses, and health-care folks who are going to the mission field. It would also provide training for pastors, missionaries, and their families to function where there are no medical facilities, especially to help them set up clinics in the field. I don't think Hank would ever have been happy working in a big medical center, only working with wealthy clients. That would have not been the real him."

"What is Hank going to call it?" Lien asked.

Amberley smiled. "It will be called the Cumberland Research Center in honor of Dr. Cumberland."

"How did you ever get him to set a date? I thought he wanted to wait until his residency was up and he was settled," Brenda asked.

"Well, strangely enough, right after showing me the drawings, he said he thought it best if we set a date while the weather was still cool and the bugs not so bad. Where that came from I don't know."

"That's wonderful, Amber, and Hank is a wonderful guy. Speaking of that, we have to get ourselves into place. Dad will be here in a couple of minutes to escort you down the stairs." Brenda helped Amberley to her feet. "Soon it will be all over but the crying."

Nineteen
No More Doubts

The old doctor's office was just an extra room built off a small, one-bedroom house in town many years ago. Rarely having seen a paintbrush through the years, the outside walls had weathered gray and were stained green with moss; the roof and sides were festooned with vines and creeper. Nearby, shaded under an ancient maple tree with a massive trunk, was a rusting Rambler sedan that burned almost as much oil as it did gasoline, the odometer having gone around several times.

Inside the office, a vintage Bakelite telephone rested on the corner of a rolltop desk in the corner, its frayed cloth cord twisted and hanging, the numbers on the rotary dialer worn clean. The untidy desk was strewn with papers, files, and scribbled notes, their sense and order known only to the man who had penned them. A prescription drug pad stained with cup rings served as a handy coaster next to a glass beaker stuffed with wooden tongue depressors, used more lately for stirring coffee than for their intended purpose. Brown, blue, and clear glass bottles of liquids and powders cluttered the shelves of the cabinet by the wall, and reference books and manuals representing decades of evolving medical knowledge collected dust on a hastily built shelf above. Antique syringes and needles soaked in a container of yellowing alcohol, and a threadbare blood pressure cuff hung from the coat rack by the door next to an old stethoscope that dangled from a brown, half-opened leather medical bag sitting on top.

The annoying rattle of the phone's clapper sounded out a steady pattern of percussive notes. Ringing persistently seven or eight times, the trailing clatter faded into silence, ignored and unanswered as though it had never rung.

Seated in his leather chair in front of the desk was a very old man. A bamboo cane with a tarnished brass ferrule worn nearly through lay across his lap. A brown and white spaniel rested her head upon his knee, breathing softly under her master's hand.

The old man, gangly in his ponderous suit, stared out the window, wholly lost in thought. The phone rang again, but the occupant of the chair doesn't stir to answer — or perhaps he didn't hear. The shadows in the room lengthened and then darkened as the old man's hand no longer moved but floated motionless above the head of his faithful friend. And as the darkness filled the chamber with unrecognizable images, the ancient warrior of the sick closed his eyes, uttering a few inaudible words — *Who will see after my poor folks?*

* * *

September seemed to mock the fleeting summertime by yellowing the greenery and ushering in the cooler nights, making them crisper, longer, clearer; sopping the grasses with heavy dew. The yellow jackets in their banded vests also knew the time—harsh little soldiers under the brighter summer sun now shunned the society of their fellows, content to languish away as hermits, to lap the sugary drops from harvested bushels of ripened fruit. Crickets of the field, mostly unnoticed in their private world of soil and grass, now warned of the frost to come, chirping loudly their somber notes under the farmer's kitchen window. The trees in the hollow along the St. Joseph River and across the fields from Hillandale Road now gloried as willing easels, displaying their canvases with flourishes of random color, splashed in the night as if by an unseen, mischievous hand.

The Bridges family sat around the supper table in honor of Hank, who was now a full-fledged doctor of medicine. With his residency completed and marriage a happy reality, having Hank home for keeps was an entirely new experience for Amberley. And although her husband was wealthy in his own right, she much admired his lack of avarice, shown in his simplicity and willingness to make a home with her on the big farm.

Amberley was happy not to be leaving Sodus, but it was still her way to visit the dark side of an issue. A momentary shadow passed by her, and she wondered if in some subtle way, Hank was remaining in Sodus only to please her. He could easily go out and make a name for himself at a large medical center or set up an elaborate practice in a big city, catering to the affluent.

Brenda often teased her because she could so easily create a problem where there had not been one before. She smiled at her silly notion and vowed to put the matter to rest forever and trust her new husband and the Lord who gave him to her. After all, her prayers had been answered, and all things had worked together for good.

Sam, with his graying temples, sat at the head of the table looking out at his family. He was reflective and content, having recently returned from North Carolina. God had blessed him, and in spite of all that had happened in his past, had allowed him to become a patriarch of sorts. Just when he desperately needed validation, he had been asked to participate in the Special Forces Q Course. He would always be the man in the tiger fatigues, even though they were now carefully preserved in moth crystals.

Brenda sat next to Joe, doting upon him, her arm embracing his with the light of love shining in her eyes. Maudie was gone, and Brenda was now the woman of the house, helping Joe keep up the farm and anticipating a family of their own.

Karl and Beth and their new baby, though not relatives, would always be treated as family. The sixty-acre plot of land, the Christmas gift from old Jeb, would give them a place to one day build a house and perhaps start a small farm of their own.

Then there was Lien, seated at the corner of the table. With all the attention recently given her older sisters and their new lives and husbands, she had gone almost unnoticed. A shadow seemed to lurk behind her sweet smile that contrasted with the day's merriment. Lien was beginning to prepare herself for the day when she would be alone in the big farmhouse. And although she was happy with her life in Sodus, she soberly understood that she must never forget her real parents, who lay in a grave at the top of the orchard hill, and the place of her birth many thousands of miles away on the other side of the world. She knew, too, that there would always be those who would define her by her Asian features first and her personhood last. Only God and time would reveal her future, but she knew that her adopted family all loved her and would always be there for her. Perhaps one day soon, she would choose to take Billy, the dusty street urchin from Sodus, and make him her own.

Sam's mind returned from the wilderness of his thoughts, and he noticed his beloved Mary staring at him. She had been God's greatest gift to him besides his relationship with the Lord Jesus, and he did not like to think what his life would have been without her. She'd always been loyal and loving and had not deserved the obstacles he had put in her path over the years. He noticed threads of silver in her reddish hair and suspected that he was responsible for most of them. When she looked at him, he knew she loved him. It had always been that way, and Sam could not love her more than he did at that moment.

The phone on the wall of the kitchen rang, always a bother when a meal was on. Lien rose to answer it.

"A moment, please," Lien said, holding the receiver to her side and looking over at Hank. "I think it's for you, Hank. They want to speak to the doctor."

The family at the table was suddenly still, and all eyes were on Hank as he took the phone from Lien. Speaking a few short words, Hank hung up the phone and looked over at Amberley. "It's the Askews, a poor family living down near the river bottom by Oxbow. It seems their girls are pretty sick. They tried to ring up Doctor Cumberland, but apparently he is not in. Since I worked with Doc and made visits with him, they know me and called here, asking that I come."

Hank turned his head and looked out the window. "I know about this family. In fact, I'm pretty familiar with all of Doc's patients after working with him for such long hours and all. The Askews are wretchedly poor country folk, too poor and proud to call an ambulance or go to the emergency room. I'd better go."

Hank disappeared upstairs and returned again with a brand-new medical bag that had been a gift from his father. Kissing Amberley on the cheek, he walked to the kitchen door, looking back at the family, whose eyes were fixed on him. Sam stood up and followed him out. "Hank? A moment?"

Clear of the kitchen door, Sam and Hank paused on the porch steps. "Son, it's been my way to stay out of my grown-up kids' lives. I know you've got a tender heart, but you're not Dr. Cumberland. He is a relic from a different time, and when he started out doctoring, this was the way it was done. Things are different now."

Hank smiled. "Thank you, sir, but somebody must go."

"Then let me say this and I'm through," Sam said softly, reaching out and putting his hand on Hank's shoulder. "Once you start attending these folks, you will not be able to easily end it. Word will get out, and they will be calling you day and night. Maybe you should talk this over with your wife, because in the long run, it will affect her too."

Hank stood silently for a moment, holding the handle of his black bag with both hands. "Dad, I appreciate what you are saying, but . . ."

"Go ahead, Hank," came Amberley's voice from the doorway behind him. "Those little girls need you. If this is what you want to do, let's do it together—no regrets, no looking back. I don't know where this will all lead, but I think Dr. Cumberland was preparing you for this all along."

Hank stared into Amberley's flashing blue eyes and then winked at her. "I'll be back as soon as I can."

THE END

The Old Sodus Series from First School Press

At Home in Old Sodus
ISBN-13: 978-0982975602
Amberley Bridges has always tried to trust God. When her alcoholic father seeks salvation through Jesus Christ, Amberley can hardly believe the wonderful changes that come to her family—but more changes, and challenges, are just around the corner. Growing up, facing bullies, and taking a stand in the classroom are just the beginning. When Amberley's family takes in two "stray cats," stubborn spitfire Brenda and Vietnamese immigrant Lien, the stage is set for the greatest tests of faith Amberley has ever known.

Life in Old Sodus
ISBN-13: 978-0982975619
Amberley and Brenda Bridges are in their junior year of high school, and life's challenges are just getting started. Whether it's working a summer job for the rich and eccentric recluse Katherine Holloway, feeling the first unforeseen glimmers of romance, or learning to take responsibility for their futures, Amberley and Brenda have their hands—and hearts—full. When their first real fight threatens to tear their friendship apart, it takes near tragedy in the form of a visit from the past to grow them into the young women they know God wants them to be—and to create a place for unexpected heroes. The continuing story of the Bridges family, *Life in Old Sodus* is the exciting sequel to *At Home in Old Sodus*.

The Big Farm in Old Sodus
ISBN-13: 978-0982975626
Running the big farm in Hipps Hollow is a bigger challenge than Sam Bridges expected it to be—especially when old farmhand Jeb Sanders retires. In the midst of farm work and the search for a good hand, Sam's family is growing up before his eyes. With college right around the corner, Brenda and Amberley must make decisions—about education, life, and love—that will set the course of their lives, while Lien faces racial prejudice for the first time and must find the strength to overcome. But it's an unexpected illness that truly puts the Bridges family to the test: do they have the faith and love to trust God even if it means losing that which they hold most dear?

Available at AMAZON in paperback and on KINDLE

The Old Sodus Series from First School Press

Grace in Old Sodus

ISBN-13: 978-0-982975640

For the Bridges family, September's legacy is one of change. This year is no exception. As Brenda embraces the hard life of a poor farmer's wife, Amberley's storybook romance is threatened by recurring illness—and her intended's seeming ambivalence about setting a wedding date. Sam, meanwhile, is coming to grips with his status as an aging warrior, a veteran without a place in the world. But it is Lien who catapults the family into crisis when a misguided vow sends her best friend into danger in the dark, forgotten woods on the edge of Old Sodus. When he goes missing, the search uncovers a decades-old mystery and brings everyone face-to-face with the grace that attends their lives.

Other Books by the Author

Mystery in the Bear Paw Mountains

ISBN-13: 978-0982975633

In the remote Bear Paw Mountains of north-central Montana, two missionaries have gone missing. Their only tracks: a distress letter written by their daughter, and rumors of a small band of Nez Perce still hiding in the mountains after the 1877 defeat of their people in the Battle of the Bear Paws. Deputy Marshal Pete Randers finds himself roped into the job of going after them. Taking with him a tenderfoot doctor's son barely saved from the hangman's noose, Pete journeys into the dangerous wilderness in search of the truth, the missionaries, and the last hope of a forgotten people.

Available at AMAZON in paperback and on KINDLE